D1564609

A CHANGE OF PLANS FOR THE YOUNGEST SON

TEXAS REDEMPTION - BOOK 4

APRIL MURDOCK

This is a work of fiction. Any references to names, characters,
organizations, places, events, or incidents are either products of the
author's imagination or are used fictitiously.

A CHANGE OF PLANS FOR THE YOUNGEST SON

TEXAS REDEMPTION - BOOK 4

APRIL MURDOCK

Everything's bigger in Texas. Even redemption.

CHAPTER ONE

Pushing a loose lock of her hair behind her ear, Kylie Cormier wrote out another few sentences for her paper on convertible interest rates in longhand. Writing her accounting essays out like this ensured that she'd be able to put her thoughts together in a more coherent manner. And since she hadn't failed to get an A yet, she believed her process must be working. Besides, doing her classwork between patrons could be disorienting, and even get her off track, so doing it old school kept her focused.

Also, doing it this way brought something familiar to her life when everything else had changed.

Peering out the glass double doors stationed in the middle of the stone façade of her parents' business location, her gaze went unfocused, her eyes only vaguely registering the trio of dogwood trees blooming along the sidewalk outside. Although Cormier's Cleaning and Alterations resided in a strip mall, whoever had contracted the landscaping had done an excellent job. The swath of green grass that separated the concrete from the parking lot pavement had been mowed just that morning, giving the air a fresh smell.

Honestly, this rental space could be considered even better than the building they'd had for twenty years down in the Big Easy.

Having moved to Dallas after living her entire life in New Orleans meant her parents' dry-cleaning business sometimes experienced significant lulls between customers. They'd recently invested in both an online ad and a radio spot, though, so hopefully things would pick up. On the bright side, Kylie could use these slower times at the counter to complete her homework. And that could only be considered a blessing.

At twenty-one, she should technically be finishing up her undergrad accounting degree, but because she'd decided to be only a part-time student for now, graduation day would likely be far into her future. Since she'd always had an analytical mind that loved math, anything having to do with numbers appealed to her. She'd had this dream of getting that degree and becoming a certified public accountant—she could even open her own business and be an entrepreneur in her own right—but this move had caused a great deal of upheaval.

Her family wouldn't have moved at all had it not been for her uncle's failing health. Her mother's brother, Kyle— Kylie's namesake—was the only surviving family member Bettina Cormier had left outside of her daughter and husband. A year ago, Kyle had developed early-onset dementia and discovered he would need full-time care. Luckily, he'd purchased top-notch insurance and had set up his long-term health plan himself, but Kylie's mom had still wanted to spend as much time with her ailing brother as possible.

Kylie understood. Her mom had always been close to her uncle despite the fifteen-year difference in their ages. Bettina wanted to be there for him while Kyle still remembered who she, her dad, and Kylie actually were.

In the six months since she'd been here in Texas, her uncle had deteriorated noticeably. At least now that they were only ten minutes from his long-term care facility, the three of them would be able to check in on him regularly. It was what family did. Family was why Kylie had moved with her mom and dad, to support them as a worker at the dry cleaners. It was why she'd transferred from the Freeman School of Business at Tulane University to the UNT (University of North Texas) School of Business there in Dallas, despite losing a handful of her college credits.

Family meant everything to Kylie. Always had. Always would.

And she knew that successful businesses all ran on a formula. Figure out what service an area might need. Provide an exemplary version of said service. Give patrons all the attention they deserved and earn their trust. Ask patrons to spread news of their positive experience with others. Advertise to a wider audience. Rinse and repeat.

As if her thoughts had summoned fresh patrons right out of thin air, the glass front door swung open, ringing the little bell her mother had hung on the inside handle. Kylie looked up to see a pair of men enter wearing expensive suits. Scrutinizing them more closely revealed that those suits were tailor-made to fit each man, which stoked her excitement. Her mother was a fabulous seamstress, and since such skills were a dying art, much of what they currently earned was due to her nimble and talented fingers.

"Hi," she greeted them brightly. "How may I help you gentlemen?"

One of the men, a guy with curly black hair that seemed to have taken over his head as it fell into his eyes, leaned an elbow on the counter. "Oh, no, sweetcheeks, this is gonna be about how *we* can help *you*."

Kylie frowned at the guy. From the second he'd opened his mouth, he'd suddenly begun to reek of the type of smarminess ever-present in the worst of used car salesmen. She crossed her arms over her chest, but before she could say anything else, Mr. Smarmy went on.

"Your business is new here, yeah?" he said in a manner that told Kylie he was already fully aware of when they'd first introduced their business to the neighborhood.

"We opened last November, yes," she said anyway, watching him with reserved caution.

"Well, this part of the city can be…" he trailed off deliberately, glancing behind him at the second man, who grinned back at him knowingly. The second man's curly yet shorter hair and similar features spoke of them being related. "How do I put this delicately? *Less than safe* if certain precautions aren't taken."

What was this? What on earth was Mr. Smarmy even talking about?

"I'm afraid I don't understand, Mr. uh…"

"Menotti. Pietro Menotti. I'm here on behalf of Viktor Menotti. Perhaps you've heard of us?"

Menotti. She played the name over in her mind. It did sound vaguely familiar, but only in the way you might remember the title of a book you'd glimpsed the spine of in the library without taking the time to pick it up and investigate further.

"I'm afraid not."

He straightened back up and put a hand to his chest as if mortally offended. "We Menottis are sort of like goodwill ambassadors here in the Big D. We provide services necessary to keep fine establishments like yours from being harassed or endangered."

"Endangered?" Kylie exclaimed before she could downplay her reaction.

Pietro threw her a predatory smile. He pulled an object out of his inner suit coat pocket, a small stick with a white wrapper on the end bearing the Dum Dum logo. Kylie had eaten plenty of those growing up. As she watched, he yanked off the waxy paper and plunged the red lollipop into his mouth, thrusting it into the side of his cheek. Then, using both hands, he took the wrapper and rolled it until the paper became a miniature ball.

"From the sharks called the Boccias," he said, clicking the candy against his teeth. "They're a group of thugs who like to prey on small businesses. How many arsons they probably responsible for, Dante?"

"Eh, in the last five years? Ten or so. And that's not even mentioning the missing people."

"Human trafficking is what they're calling it on the news," Pietro corrected the other man's terminology, effecting an expression of disgust. "Ugly, brutal stuff. There's been a lot of armed robberies with shootings, too. Nasty business. I'd hate to see Cormier's Cleaning and Alterations exposed to such... unpleasantness."

Who these men really were hit her right in the gut, and all at once she remembered hearing each name in association with the other on the news. The Menottis and the Boccias were organized crime families. For whatever random reason, her parents' little cleaning establishment had somehow drawn the attention of the *mob*.

Good gracious!

Kylie felt a strong compulsion to run from the front counter, collect both her parents, and hide in a bunker somewhere. She didn't, though. Despite her instincts to flee, she understood that any show of weakness with these people would be an error she might never recover from. Down in New Orleans, she'd been bullied throughout her middle school years. It'd taken her standing up to her bullies during her sophomore year in high school to finally be rid of them.

And since these Menottis struck her as bullies, she stood her ground.

"We're not fans of unpleasantness either," she said, thrusting her hands into the front pockets of her jeans to conceal how much they were trembling. "Which is why we like building up a rapport with the local law enforcement."

Back home, a couple of the street officers who'd patrolled their section of town had become trusted friends.

Pietro leaned in again, quirking up one side of his mouth. He removed the lollipop and gestured at her with it. "I could tell that you were one smart cookie when we walked in here. The thing about law enforcement here in Dallas is that honorable as they no doubt are, there still might be a certain percentage of them on our payroll."

Might be? Yeah, right. Apparently veiled threats were this guy's forte. If Kylie and her parents couldn't depend on the cops to save them, that left these guys. These clearly reprehensible wise guys. For the first time, Kylie felt real regret at their decision to relocate here, even if they couldn't have had any idea this would happen. She tightened the hands in her pockets into fists and squared her shoulders.

No signs of weakness, Kylie. Absolutely none.

"How abouts we make you a deal?" Pietro continued. "We Menottis protect you and yours from whatever the Boccias might attempt to inflict upon you, and you agree to pay us a small stipend for services rendered."

"How small a stipend?"

"Not much. Five thou a month should do it. At least for now. A pittance, really," Pietro answered, looking smug. But Kylie's anger flared.

Five thousand dollars might be a pittance to Mr. Smarmy, but to her family, it'd nearly break the bank. They hadn't had the chance to build up their customer base yet, and they'd also just reinvested most of last month's funds into advertising. Kylie had no clue where they might come up with that sort of cash. If they even made that much of a profit in the first place. And here was the clincher. They shouldn't have to.

"I'll have to pass that along to the owners," she informed the two men, putting on her bravest face.

Pietro pushed back from the counter, his posture steeped in the sort of arrogance that came from knowing he had someone between a rock and a hard place. His smile widened, and Kylie wished she could shout at him to leave, even if she didn't dare. "You do that, sweetcheeks. Then, we'll be back to solidify the terms of our generous arrangement."

The instant she saw the backs of the men, Kylie pivoted and dashed to the back, passing beneath the electric conveyor belt filled with people's plastic-covered dry cleaning, past the massive spinning dryers and washing machines. In a little room with a sewing machine was her mother and near the back was her dad. Since some of those washers and dryers were in use, the noise they made blocked out all other sound but their rhythmic circular roar. She could basically guarantee that neither of them would've heard any of what had just transpired.

Kylie seized her father's arm and brought him into the sewing room, closing the heavy wooden door that separated her mom's domain from the rest of the place. She needed to inform them of the conversation that had been forced on her without alarming them to the point of panic. She took in her father, Reggie, standing there all stalwart with concern lining his face, his aqua blue eyes—ones she'd inherited from him—watching her alertly.

Then she focused on her mother, whose beautiful chestnut hair had started to become shot through with gray. How was it that Kylie had noticed only this second how much gray there now was? Her mother pulled her sweater tightly around her despite the heat and humidity perpetually present in any dry-cleaning facility. The woman was perpetually cold.

"Kylie, what is it?" her father prompted her, and with a deep breath that went all the way to her diaphragm, she spoke.

"We have a big problem."

CHAPTER TWO

TONY TOOK A BITE OF HIS LASAGNA, REGARDING HIS FATHER, brother, uncle, and cousins out of the corner of one eye. They all sat at the huge mahogany table—the surface polished so astutely that he could see his reflection—eating their meal. Positioned at the head of that table was his father, Viktor. Behind him stood an old-fashioned woodburning fireplace constructed of traditional maroon brickwork. This, as per usual, was a business meeting masquerading as a family dinner.

The conspicuous absence of any of the female members of said family spoke to this. Though in his immediate *famiglia*, there were no longer any women to attend, even if they hadn't been kept in the dark as to the true nature of what the men were up to. Elliana Minichiello Menotti, his beloved *mamma*, had passed away a year ago last week, a fact he continued to grieve.

Still, knowing it was what she would've wanted, he'd tried to go on with his life. Prior to losing his mother, Tony hadn't taken much of an interest in his clan's less-than-legal pursuits. Studying with private tutors, he'd focused on creating charcoal portraits and landscapes as well as playing the violin, his mother's favorite instrument. He'd gained all of his education through such tutors, only socializing with family members or close-as-family friends. It'd been a solitary existence, and one he felt an increasing need to branch out from.

Hence, his presence tonight.

In fact, tonight he would make his first move.

Over the last eight months or so, Tony had attempted to learn the ins and outs of what precisely it was that the Menottis did. He'd sat in on meetings, listening to discussions about money changing hands and about just how far the Menotti's territory extended throughout the city of Dallas. It'd been his fourth meeting before he'd heard anything specific about their underhanded business practices. Now, when his cousins Pietro and Dante bragged about adding yet another mark to their list of "taxable" businesses, he knew what they were referring to.

He might be the smallest minnow in their fishpond, but his cousins barely ranked above him. Those two... well, they couldn't be considered the brightest colors in the crayon box. His brother, Alessandro, on the other hand, had a sharp intelligence. More than that, Sandro had common sense and good instincts. He knew how to read a room in such a way that he could be convincing without pushing too hard. Tony had always looked up to him.

Viktor Menotti, their father, tended to rule with a much heavier hand. The sledgehammer approach compared to Sandro's scalpel. As the patriarch of their *famiglia*, Viktor wielded all the power and made all the major decisions. Unlike his *mamma*, Tony didn't feel especially close to his father. He never had. Which was the main reason why he'd abandoned all his creative endeavors to go to work as a cog in the Menotti Crime Syndicate machine.

Waiting until his father had stopped speaking so he could take a cheesy bite of his meal, Tony swallowed down his nerves and stood. "*Papà*, I would like to take my place in the organization."

Viktor barely offered him a glance. "That so?"

"Yes."

Cutting through the flat pasta noodles with great deliberation, Viktor took another bite, chewing thoughtfully. "You have only started to be here for the meetings recently," his father pointed out.

Tony nodded, squaring his shoulders and stiffening his spine. Now that he was on his feet, it felt as if a spotlight was shining upon him. Of course, that was his intent. "For eight full months now. I believe I could be an asset to you. To all of us." Pietro made a noise behind Tony; it might've been a snicker. Ignoring it, Tony plowed on. "I am a man. I'm capable and willing."

"You are a boy, Antonio."

"I'm twenty-two."

"Exactly," Viktor sliced into the lasagna again. "You're too young."

"Sandro was indoctrinated far younger," Tony countered, careful to keep his voice strong despite being nervous.

Any hint of whining would make him sound like the very child his father had already accused him of being. This was his only shot. His father didn't give second chances. He'd just taken another breath to support his argument further when his father cut him off.

"Your brother is the eldest, and he also always showed an interest in and a devotion to serving his *famiglia*. It is his duty and responsibility to take on the mantle when I am gone. *He* is the heir. You are not."

"So because I'm nothing but the backup son my contribution is worthless?" Tony regretted the words the moment they left his mouth. They'd been spoken in frustration and not a little bit of recklessness.

For a second, an eerie and foreboding silence filled their opulent dining room, then Viktor's voice bounced off the walls like cannon fire as he threw his glass into the brick fireplace behind him. "You will not disrespect me, boy!"

His father's yell had been like a lightning strike, flashing vividly, setting everything afire, and leaving devastation in its wake. Tony dragged his eyes from his father's cold and irate features to peer at the table. This was the expected display of deference. "I meant no disrespect, *Papà*. I apologize. Sincerely."

"Sit," Viktor ordered him next. "For now, the matter is closed."

Comprehending that he'd lost this go-around, Tony did as his father wished. Defiance would not be tolerated, even though as his biological son, technically Tony should've ranked higher than anyone other than the patriarch or Sandro. Not that Tony cared about rank. Sandro had long since earned his place, and Tony had no desire to supplant him. What Tony really wanted was something he'd never received from Viktor Menotti.

The man's attention. The man's consideration. The man's love.

The dinner went on and Tony was relegated to the background once again. He sat there feeling bitter, but he kept his mouth shut. Saying more would only make his situation worse.

"Things went well on one of the newer locations down on Campbell," Pietro spoke up loudly, as if oblivious to the tension still present in the room. "Should be easy pickings."

Tony peeked in his father's direction, but the older man made no indication that he'd heard Pietro's drivel as he shoveled more food into his mouth. This didn't stop his cousin, though.

"It's a dry cleaners. And the clerk there is a pretty young thing."

"Yeah," Dante picked up the narrative. "Didn't meet the owners, but if they give us any hassles, we could take the girl and use her as a bargaining chip."

"You didn't meet the owners?" Viktor whipped his head up all at once. "Why not?"

"Uh…" was Pietro's brilliant response. Typical.

Viktor threw his fine linen napkin down over his plate which was still half full. "How many times do I have to instruct you two on proper procedure? You don't rely on underlings when it comes to communications. Always demand to speak with the highest person on the totem pole when negotiating prices. *Always*."

Pietro and Dante both nodded up and down continuously. They looked like a couple of bobble heads. Even Tony, as green as he was, knew this. He doubted his cousins would retain the knowledge regardless. As his father had stated, this wasn't the first time they'd been warned about this.

"Antonio," Viktor turned his formidable attention back to Tony. "You wanted to be more involved."

"I do, sir."

"Then go with these two next week on their rounds. I'm putting it on you to make certain they follow instructions without deviation. Can I trust you to do this?"

"Absolutely, *Papà*." Tony attempted to quell just how excited he was, which proved challenging, but he somehow managed.

"Very well. Report to Alessandro when you return."

The night had not gone as planned, but he'd still gotten what he wanted. Tony stayed on cloud nine through the rest of dinner. Once his father left the table and disappeared into his suite on the opposite side of the house, Sandro addressed his cousins.

"You two, Tweedledee and Tweedledum, hightail it. I need to speak to my brother."

Sulkily, Pietro and Dante complied, the elder of the two unwrapping and thrusting one of his ever-present lollipops in his mouth as he did, despite having only moments before finished a large meal. They dared not rebel against the heir. That'd be almost as much of an infringement as defying the patriarch himself. After waiting for their footfalls to disappear into another part of the mansion, Sandro approached Tony, grabbing his arm.

"What was that?" his brother asked him, his gaze more anxious than short tempered.

Tony furrowed his brows. "What was what?"

"*That*. That thing with *Papà*. You volunteering for service, as it were."

"It's time for me to step up, that's all."

"Step up?" Sandro sounded incredulous. "Had you annoyed *Papà* any more than you did, he might've throttled you." Tony said nothing. He knew his brother was right. Still, since everything had turned out like he'd wanted it to, he couldn't complain. "Why are you wanting to get your hands dirty all of a sudden? What about your art? Your music?"

"My art and music will always be there, but right now, I want to demonstrate that I'm a true Menotti. I want to prove my worth."

Sandro threw an arm around his shoulders. "You have always been worthy. You needn't change your original career trajectory. I have it handled, which means you can do whatever you wish."

"What I wish is to be of service."

"You never felt that way before."

"I feel that way now. What's it to you?" Tony demanded to know, feeling more and more offended by his brother's interrogation. Didn't Sandro believe him capable of the task?

Sandro blew out a breath. "I don't want you hurt. This job... our *famiglia*... what we do can be dangerous."

He glanced down at his left hand and the scar that resided there. About six months prior, his brother had been grazed by a bullet, though Tony didn't know the specific details. The tissue left behind was raised and uneven, the color an angry pink. Tony thought of it like a badge of courage, proof that Sandro was unafraid of anything. The wound hadn't even slowed him down. Tony wanted the chance to display his own bravery in the same way. Why couldn't his brother see that?

"I want to become an authentic and fully fledged member of this *famiglia*, someone our father actually values. I want to be like you."

Sandro frowned. "No, you don't."

"Yes, I do. I know you feel protective of me, Sandro, but I'd like to help." He'd do anything for Sandro, but in truth, he'd been hoping to forge a better connection with Viktor. He was, after all, the only parent Tony or Sandro had left.

"I'd feel better if you helped in another way, *fratello*. Some of what I do... I'd rather you not be exposed to it."

"But see, that's what I mean," Tony protested, shrugging his brother's arm off him. Sandro was five years his senior, and sometimes he behaved more like a parent than a sibling. "You're acting like I'm a baby."

"I know you're not a baby, Antonio." Sandro sighed, pushing his hand through his thick, dark hair. Unlike Tony, Sandro had inherited his father's black hair, though they both had their mother's lighter eyes. "You're a grown man capable of making your own decisions. But you're also a good man with a kind heart, and if you become more involved in the organization, that might no longer be the case."

Tony scoffed. He loved his brother, he truly did, but he was also sick of Sandro treating him with kid gloves. "You're a good man, and you're as involved in the organization as it's possible to be."

Sandro paled, the light going out behind his eyes. His expression became stark, as if someone had just told him horrible news. "I'm not as good as you think I am."

Then, without further explanation, his older brother burst from the room, leaving Tony to stare in confusion at the absence he'd left behind.

CHAPTER THREE

DESPITE KYLIE COUCHING WHAT HAD HAPPENED IN THE gentlest terms she possible could, her folks still flipped out. Well, maybe flipped out sounded too extreme. It wasn't like they'd yanked out their hair and dived through a plate glass window or anything. But they were both on edge. Or tenterhooks. Or some other descriptive word Kylie couldn't seem to access from the recesses of her brain at the moment. Ever since those Menotti thugs had shown up with their horrendous "offer," neither her mom nor her dad would leave Kylie alone up front anymore.

This meant that their overall business productivity started to suffer a little as a result. Or in the case of her mom's seamstress work, a lot.

It wasn't difficult for Kylie to be the one to go to the back and run the washing machines and dryers. She'd known how to do that since shortly after she'd started third grade. She could press out clothing, too, iron all the wrinkles out until the fabric looked brand spanking new. But alterations and sewing took not only time but skill, and since she didn't actually possess that skill? Well, it meant within a relatively brief period of time, there began to be a backlog.

Fortunately, the backlog hadn't grown too overwhelming so far.

Her mother had taken to bringing certain pieces she could alter with a needle and thread out with her to the front. Still, it was a concern. Because the three of them had to figure out what they could do about being blackmailed. The day after it'd happened, none of them had slept. Kylie knew this because she'd gone downstairs for some chamomile and found each of her parents up. Her dad had been watching a baseball game with his headphones, and her mom had simply paced the length of the kitchen and dining room combo nonstop.

This did nothing to help soothe Kylie's own frazzled nerves.

After collecting her tea, she'd slipped right back upstairs. She needed advice, so although it was after midnight, she texted her best friend back in New Orleans.

Kylie: You still up?

Shelley: You know it.

This didn't surprise Kylie. Her bestie had always been a night owl. She hit Shelley's name on her favorites list.

"Hey, what's up?"

"Oh, you're not going to believe what happened yesterday."

"Something juicy?" Shelley sounded delighted but delighted wasn't how Kylie would ever feel about all this.

"Something *scary*. Your little sister isn't around, is she? I don't want anyone else hearing this. This is some next-level stuff, Shell. For real."

"Let me just close my door." Kylie heard a creak, then silence. "Okay, you're freaking me out now. Spill it."

"I'm pretty sure I was threatened by the mob yesterday morning."

"You were? *Why*?"

"Well, not me personally, but Cormier's was. These men in dark suits came in and told us we relocated to a dicey and crime-ridden neighborhood. To keep us safe, they want five thousand a month."

"What? Please tell me you're not serious."

"I'm as serious as a heart attack, sweetie. Mom and Dad are terrified. *I'm* terrified. But I'm really mad, too, you know?" The more she said, the faster she spoke. "It's just so unfair. Where's the justice? We can't go to the police because apparently some of them are on these dudes' payroll. If they're telling the truth, anyway. But I think they are telling the truth because of how menacing they were."

"Did they threaten you with weapons?"

"You mean like guns? No. Not overtly. Though those jackets of theirs might've been covering them up. I mean, Dad has his hunting rifles and things, but I feel like shooting at these guys would only make things worse. I don't know," Kylie ended on a hopeless groan.

Shelley stayed quiet for a minute, but Kylie knew what this meant. Her friend was thinking, trying to come up with a solution. The thing about Shelley was she was a little tiny thing at 4'11, but the woman was spunky. She didn't take anything off of anybody and never had. Also, she had Cajun roots and was smart as a whip, and not just the book smart kind, either. She had good instincts about people. The best.

"Ky?"

"Yeah?"

"What were the men's names?"

"M something. Monetti? Mikasa?"

"Was it Menotti?" Shelley asked.

"That's it."

"Did they mention the Boccias?"

"I have this really bad feeling about how you knew that," Kylie admitted.

"It's just that Daddy printed a news story about those two groups a month or two ago." Shelley's father was a news reporter down in the Big Easy, but he did stories from all over the country. "Those two families are suspected of being part of the Italian mafia. They may have ties that go back to the original crime families in Chicago—think of people like Al Capone. This could be bad, Ky. Really, truly bad."

"We're trying to figure out what to do."

"Okay, I'm at my laptop searching for that story…" There was a pause as Shelley probably scrolled. "Here it is. Yeah, it says that the Menottis were rumored to be less violent than the Boccias, at least according to rumor. It's hard to substantiate stuff like this because anyone honestly affiliated with it is either too loyal or too afraid to talk."

"What, so like the Menottis are better to deal with than the other thugs?" Kylie asked, hoping for some clarification.

"It's hard to say, and I don't know that I'd put it like that. But they appear to have less of a rap sheet, anyway. So since this is about the lesser of two evils, maybe do what they say?" Shelley's advice came out sounding more like a question. "That might be the safest way to handle it."

"Okay. I'll tell Mom and Dad what you said."

Kylie did. In fact, over the next few days, she and her parents did almost nothing *but* discuss their current predicament. Ultimately, they decided that if they couldn't pay the "protection money," they would just throw themselves on the Menottis' mercy. No use attempting to get blood from a turnip, right? Kylie just hoped they'd show her family some compassion, even if they were bonafide members of a crime organization.

As time passed, Kylie and her parents became more and more antsy. While she prayed that the Menottis would just go away and stay that way, she couldn't imagine them making such a threat without meaning it.

Kylie had been working on a paper for the past three days —her concentration had been nonexistent, wonder why— for her Advanced Global Economics course. She'd been trying to write the first paragraph for what had to be the twenty-seventh time when her mother's bell rang again. Outside it was another beautiful day. Tufts of what was likely to be dandelion fluff flew through the warm air, and pollen coated everything in sight in a light, sticky sheen of yellow.

A full week had gone by since those two men had sauntered through their door, and now it was three other men who had materialized. They weren't the same men, but they had a similar look about them. Dark suits that were tailor-made, this time of the three-piece variety. Expensive haircuts. Polished dress shoes. Since her father was at her side, she gave him a small shake of her head to indicate that these men were different. Sadly, that was as much as she could safely communicate.

Her father addressed them. "What can we do for you?"

"You can empty your till and bring up anything you have in your safe," the front man stated in a surprisingly high-pitched voice, his eyes narrowed. Those eyes were this pale gray color, almost like silver, but they were cold, too. Kylie felt chilled just looking at him despite the springlike weather outside. He wore a scarlet red tie that reminded her of blood.

"But we haven't made five thousand in profits yet," her father protested, and Kylie felt an icy dread flow through the marrow of her bones. Granted, it was only the fourteenth of the month, but would they wait? Or would they insist on taking what they'd already warned them they'd come for? If their business couldn't provide the right amount, would they take their retribution out on them, nevertheless?

"Five grand?" one of the other men said, this one in a flashy emerald green tie. "Who said anything about five grand?"

"Your other…" her dad seemed to struggle to come up with a polite enough term. "Associates. The ones who came last week."

Scarlet Tie cursed under his breath. "Are you saying the Menottis were here?"

"The Menottis, yes," Kylie couldn't keep from chiming in. She couldn't stand by and watch without doing something to assist her father. If she could talk their way out of this, she would. Even if it meant making certain sacrifices.

"I told you they'd claim this property. Technically, it's on their side of the border," the third man hissed out to his compatriots, sounding put out. Were they about to get into a fight?

"Shut it," Scarlet Tie barked at the other two men, who immediately went silent. He took a pace forward, and so did the other two men, all three of them moving their suit jackets back on one side of their hips in unison. On each one of those hips was a visible leather holster, and inside the holsters were pistols. Big ones. Through her terror, Kylie had an errant thought.

So that's why people referred to that color as gunmetal gray.

Was she losing her mind? She couldn't lose it, though, not right now. Not with her dad in the line of fire.

"So, here's the deal," Scarlet Tie went on. "We're going to let you keep your little stock of coin and cash for now, but next time, if you don't immediately pony up, we're far less likely to be so forgiving."

Neither Kylie nor her father made a move. They didn't even glance at one another again. Instead, Kylie kept her dad in her peripheral vision as she watched those three men back out toward their door. Before they could make it all the way out, a pack of teenage boys wheeled by on skateboards, the sound of those rubber wheels on cement making enough noise to draw the thugs' attention.

Kylie gasped as all three men put their hands on their weapons as if getting ready to draw them on those innocent skateboarders. Just how awful was this whole scene going to get? But then, the boys disappeared around the corner, and the thugs resumed their exit. Once the men were fully out the door, Kylie ran to her father, and each of them watched the armed mobsters as the three of them went on alert.

Confused as to the reason for this new posturing, Kylie released herself from her dad's arms and moved far enough to the side to see what might be going on. Another car had pulled up into the parking lot, a big, black Cadillac Escalade.

"Someone else is here," she whispered.

"Another customer?"

"I don't know. I hope not." After witnessing the near run-in those thugs had had with the skater kids, she didn't know what they'd do if more blameless bystanders accidentally became involved.

"Kylie, get back from there," her father told her, his hands shaking. "In fact, go join your mother in her sewing room. I don't want you getting hurt."

"I don't think we can hide from these people, Dad. They don't strike me as the sort of folks who would just let us go."

"These Menottis are horrible," he observed, but she shook her head.

"I don't know that today's men were Menottis. Not the same ones, anyway. These guys were different. More aggressive. But if they are a part of the same group, why would they insist on 'protection money' only to turn around and threaten to straight up rob from us like they were doing some sort of heist?" Something they hadn't actually gone through with now that she thought about it.

Her father came up and stood between her and the clear glass entrance as if to at least shield her should things turn sideways. "Maybe they were from that other group. The Boccias or whoever," he suggested.

Now that did make sense. Maybe this was precisely what the Menottis had warned them against. Maybe paying those first two men their "fee" would keep the more aggressive of the two crime families from storming in like they owned the place. Of course, that was assuming that the Menottis were any less dangerous, and they had zero chance of knowing if that was true or not until it was too late.

There was a clacking noise of a car door being shut, and Kylie edged around her father to try to see what might be occurring right there on their front step. Another man had

31

emerged from the Escalade, one she hadn't met that first time. This one had lighter brown hair, and unlike the other two men who'd come across as smarmy as used car salesmen, this man's stance seemed to be shrewder and all business.

Also, he was drop-dead gorgeous. She could tell that at twenty paces.

Still, she didn't relax a muscle. Because the look Gorgeous tossed at the other three men could not be considered friendly. Not by any estimation. They exchanged words she couldn't hear, and then the two men she had met that first time around departed from the Escalade and stationed themselves at Gorgeous' side. Which meant whatever was about to happen would likely boil down to one thing.

A showdown.

CHAPTER FOUR

Tony FELT A COMBINATION OF DETERMINATION AND exhilaration as he stalked through the Menottis' mansion. Their estate was quite a sight to behold as it took up a full five square acres, and his grandfather, Viktor's *papà*, had spared no expense to make it as grand and magnificent as possible.

Their attached ten-car garage was no exception.

Tony passed by a menagerie of vehicles, all of which were black, expensive, finely tuned, and nondescript. Blending in had always been one of the priorities of his *famiglia*, partly due to the nature of their activities and partly because they believed being overly ostentatious was the calling card of amateurs. He and Sandro were raised knowing an extensive list of things that you did and did not do.

The Menotti protocols.

For example, you didn't go anywhere without being dressed for the occasion, preferably better dressed than anyone else. You didn't curse in front of the fairer sex or children. You didn't fail to be polite to anyone while in the public eye. You *did* always respect your elders, most especially the patriarch. You obeyed your mother. Unless you were ill, you always cleaned your plate at mealtimes. And if certain events dictated the need for violence, you only ever wielded that tool when no other alternative could be utilized.

If crimes were committed, then they were to be conducted behind closed doors whenever possible. There was a standing edict to give things at least the appearance of looking ethical and legal, even if just for propriety's sake. Since Tony hadn't been fully ensconced in the lifestyle until later in his life, he could pick out these inconsistencies for what they were, but they didn't bother him too much. Not most of the time, anyway. For him, becoming a Menotti in both name and deed was about one thing.

His father's approval.

And he'd do whatever need be to acquire it.

Sliding behind the wheel of a Black Raven Cadillac Escalade, this year's model, of course, he waited as Pietro and Dante joined him.

"But I said shotgun," Dante complained like a prepubescent teen as Pietro jumped into the passenger seat, smirking around his lollipop stick. In reality, his cousins were both older than Tony was. Pietro had turned twenty-five last month while Dante was twenty-four, yet they each acted like immature children half the time.

"Quit whining," Tony chastised, rolling his eyes.

"But I called it," Dante continued. "It's not right when I'm the one who called it."

For heaven's sake.

"Just climb in, Dante. You're acting like a toddler."

"Yeah," Pietro made fun of his brother in a singsong voice. "You're acting like a toddler."

"You're no better," Tony snapped, fed up. "*Papà* didn't assign this job to me so I could play like I'm your babysitter."

"We don't need a babysitter," Dante said, sounding indignant.

"Could've fooled me," Tony muttered, mostly to himself. The nonsense he put up with.

The thing about his two cousins was that his aunt and uncle had raised them completely differently to the way he and Sandro had been brought up. Sandro had spent the majority of his youth at their father's side learning the ins and outs of keeping the books—two sets of them—maintaining order, being taught how to demand respect, as well as all of the less savory aspects of running an organized crime syndicate. Meanwhile, Tony had been tutored in all the classical arts, most of his days spent in the company of his mother when he wasn't training.

Both the two Menotti sons did spend considerable time with one another as well. As youngsters, their relationship had usually been one of a solicitous older brother protecting his little sibling. Tony used to appreciate it, even. But now, his brother's need to put up a wall of safety and defense around him was getting in his way.

Their mansion resided near the southernmost outskirts of the city, and as he motored by the zoo to see the lit-up globe of the Reunion Tower observation deck in the distance, he mentally prepared himself to face a multitude of possibilities. He couldn't be certain of what he'd find when they arrived at the dry-cleaning business—his cousins liked to exaggerate with these types of situations —but he hoped they hadn't messed things up too badly. One ability he'd been born with was negotiation skills. His tutors and his mother used to tease him about this.

When it'd been time to stop playing the violin to come to dinner, he'd say, "I have this piece of music—or artwork canvas or portrait—almost figured out, *Mamma*. May I have just five more minutes?" He'd continue to put it off like this until his meal had turned stone cold.

He figured that if he could talk his dear mother and his various tutors into doing what he wanted, it shouldn't be much of a stretch to convince others to follow suit, too. That was his plan, anyway.

The first wrench in this plan came the instant he pulled up in front of Cormier's Cleaning and Alterations. Why? Because he recognized the older Lincoln Town Car he'd coasted in next to. The Boccias favored these cars because their Don preferred what he called classic vehicles in his organization. Another pure giveaway as to the vehicle's owner came in the form of Giovanni, Gregorio, and Luca Boccia, the three men stomping out the front door just as a group of teenagers passed by on skateboards.

"Good afternoon, gentlemen," Tony greeted them smoothly. Sandro had pointed these men out to him more than once, though more to warn him to stay away from them than for training purposes.

Giovanni, the head Boccia as well as the heir, spoke up, his hand flattening down his bright red tie.

"And who might you be?"

"Oh, so sorry I didn't introduce myself formally." He thrust out a hand. "Antonio Menotti."

"You're the Menotti second born?"

Smiling while measuring them up, he raised his hands as if in surrender. "Guilty as charged."

"I didn't know you were part of your family's machinations."

"Well, I am," he said simply, not going any further into an explanation.

"We heard that your mother passed away last year. Our most sincere condolences," Giovanni said, and for the first time, Tony's hackles rose. There was nothing sincere about the tone of his voice as he spoke, and that made him fume internally. How dare this man disrespect his dearly departed *mamma*? Still, he didn't give himself away.

"Thank you. I know she is smiling down on me from heaven. She was a saint, and now, she truly is an angel."

"Yeah, yeah. I'm sure," Giovanni responded, a gleam in his silver eyes.

Tony bit his tongue so he wouldn't mouth off, but unfortunately, Pietro and Dante had chosen that second to go from standing near the Escalade to encroaching from behind him. They stopped, flanking him.

"Yo, these boys giving you any trouble, Tony?" Pietro asked, flexing his biceps rather blatantly, his mouth for once lollipop-free.

"Yeah, these boys giving you trouble?" Dante echoed his brother's nearly identical sentiment, doing the same muscle flex.

Seriously?

"I'm good, *cuginos. Grazie.* You know the Boccias, don't you? Giovanni, Gregorio, and Luca?"

Pietro nodded his head. "Yeah, we know 'em."

Giovanni, for his part, squinted over at Tony appraisingly. Perhaps he wondered how Tony knew them on sight while they'd had no idea who *he* was. Tony found he liked having an advantage over these men, but he figured he shouldn't take it for granted.

"We were just having a bit of conversation to get to know each other better," Tony went on. "Now, gentlemen, if you'll excuse us, we have some chores to complete. A man's work is never done these days, as I'm sure you already know."

The Boccias regarded him and his cousins carefully, sizing them up. For a moment, Tony wondered if they'd be foolish enough to start an all-out gunfight right there in broad daylight. This strip mall may not be on the most beaten of paths, but it wasn't that isolated, either. Vehicles and pedestrians were visible, and while few had come close during their encounter, that didn't mean that they wouldn't pose a much more significant problem should their standoff erupt with bullets.

In fact, over the past six months, Pietro and Dante had been training him in marksmanship. They might not have the highest of IQs, but the two could certainly hit targets with great accuracy when they chose to do so. Tony supposed it came with the territory. And now, though his jacket obscured his weapon far better than the Boccias camouflaged theirs, he'd become just as accurate.

Deciding to make a gambit himself, he pivoted away from the Boccias and stepped up to the entrance of the dry cleaners. He didn't look to see Giovanni or his brothers' reactions, but he kept all his other senses attuned to their actions. When he heard three car doors slam, followed by a Lincoln peeling out of its parking space, he inwardly breathed a sigh of relief. He gave no outward indication, though. Instead, he pushed the glass door open until a bell rang and entered the establishment.

Once inside, he blinked to adjust his vision from bright sunshine to the dimmer artificial lighting and spotted two people. An older graying man with a slight paunch, and a fresh-faced girl around his age with aqua blue eyes, both of their complexions blanched colorless. What had the Boccias done to them?

"Hello," Tony spoke into the tension-laced silence, coming all the way in. Pietro and Dante stood behind him. "Are you two all right?"

Just as he said these words, another older woman came on the scene, looking surprised to see him. "Um…" She pivoted around to see her other coworkers. "Kylie? Reggie? What is it?"

The girl, Kylie, answered, her eyes on Tony. "We just received another visit, Mom. Were those your men?"

"No. Those men were from the Boccia clan."

"They were about to rob us until they saw you drive up," Kylie added.

"Those no-good, sorry—" Dante started to mouth off, and Tony hastily shut him down.

"Dante. That's enough. Why don't you and Pietro go outside and secure the perimeter? Make sure they didn't leave someone behind to cause trouble." Then, after his cousins strutted back out, Tony gave one hundred percent of his attention to the people behind the counter. "Please excuse my cousin's outburst. There is no love lost between my *famiglia* and the Boccias, I'm afraid."

"Your cousins came in here last week and told us we had to pay five thousand dollars in 'protection' money a month. So how is your family any better than theirs?" Kylie asked boldly, making her mother wave at her to hush.

Tony felt impressed by this girl's audacity, even if he did notice that she shook slightly as she spoke.

"The truth is, my *famiglia* is a business. We make our presence known in this part of Dallas to keep the peace between us and our rivals."

"The Boccias," she said.

"Precisely. Unfortunately, this section of the city runs parallel to their territory, and even though technically, it is under our, shall we say, *jurisdiction*, they do like to challenge the more borderline properties. Such as this one. I can assure you, however, that will no longer be the case since we have staked our claim. The Boccias will not darken your doorstep again."

"What about the money?" the older woman asked. "What if we cannot provide it?"

"Forgive me, *signora*, but let me make some proper introductions. I'm Antonio Menotti, and please call me Tony, if you'd like. May I have your names? I'd like to conduct business properly with all of you." Tony smiled at her.

"Reggie Cormier," the man spoke up. "My wife is Bettina, and my daughter is Kylie."

"And you three own this establishment?"

"My wife and I are the legal owners, yes."

"Lovely, and you, *bellisima*?" he addressed Kylie.

"I help out as an employee," she answered, crossing her arms over her chest. He liked how she wore simple clothing. Small gold hoops in her ears. A matching herringbone bracelet on her wrist. Dark jeans with a nice but fitted blouse that brought out the blue in her eyes, which had fire behind them. Soft, medium-brown hair that waved to just beneath her shoulders. Yes, very attractive, indeed.

"All right. I believe your *mamma's* concern was about providing the money for us. Is that correct?"

"We're new here," Reggie chimed in, showing his backbone. "And we'd rather not be hassled by anyone."

"Understandable. And you worry you will not make enough, yes?"

All three Cormiers nodded.

"Well, I am happy to negotiate a compromise. What if we waive the first month's fee in a divinely fair exchange?"

"What sort of exchange?" Reggie asked, pursing his lips.

"Let's say I lower the rate of your… payments in exchange for something else. Something you can afford."

"What might that be?" Bettina asked.

"Just time," Tony explained. "A brief amount of time. A date, if you will, that I would spend with your daughter."

CHAPTER FIVE

"NO!" BOTH OF HER PARENTS CRIED OUT AT ONCE.

"You will not kidnap our daughter," her mom seized her, stuffing Kylie into her arms.

"Now, now, I did not mention any such thing. Why are you panicking?" Tony seemed puzzled as he lifted one hand in a placating gesture. Kylie could hear no deception in his voice. He sounded like he meant it. "I mean your daughter no harm, none whatsoever. I'm talking about a single date, innocent and utterly aboveboard. Perhaps a meal. All I really want is time to speak to her, get to know her. This partnership between our two *famiglias* will be long-lasting, and I want us all to be friends in good standing."

"So, all I would have to do is go out with you?" Kylie asked, but her mother literally put her hand over her daughter's mouth.

"Absolutely not, Kylie," her mom hissed at her, her voice uneven.

At the same time, her dad roared, "*Over my dead body!*"

Formally, Tony Menotti took his right hand and placed it over his heart. "I give you my word that I will act with nothing but good manners and propriety. My *mamma* raised me to be a gentleman, and I would never do her a disservice, *signore* and *signora*."

Internally, Kylie felt conflicted. But she didn't let herself show it. What good was the word of a mafia member? Even if he did come across as delightfully charming? And sincere. Despite being who he was, her instincts weren't telling her to back off like they did with some people. Mr. Smarmy she wouldn't go near with a ten-foot pole. With Mr. Scarlet Tie, the pole would have to be even longer.

Yet she didn't feel that way with this Tony guy; if anything, she felt curious.

Still, she did recollect the stories she'd heard growing up, particularly the one about the wolf in sheep's clothing. Was that what Tony Menotti was? Or was he willing to extend to her a genuine offer that would help her family get out of this mess, or at least lessen the impact on their financial bottom line? Her father's words haunted her then. "Over his dead body" might actually happen if the Boccias had their way. And she could never allow that to happen.

"Can we think about it?" Kylie asked, trying to buy some time.

"Of course, *bellisima*. I shall take my leave. And in the meantime, Cormier's Cleaning and Alternations is under our protection." After making this lofty announcement, he left.

"Kylie Alexandra, under no circumstances are you to even consider going out with that man," her mother ordered her. Obviously, she didn't trust Tony Menotti. It wasn't like Kylie could blame her too much. Still, she had to make her case.

"What else can we do?"

"Something else," her father put in. "We'll think of something else."

"Have we thought of something else in a week of sleepless nights and brainstorming?" she pointed out.

"It doesn't matter," her mom said. "We'll pull up stakes again before we let anything happen to you."

"But what if he wasn't lying, Mom? What if I spent a couple of hours eating out with him and he either lowered or erased our payments?"

"No," was all her mother said, staunchly.

"Then what about Uncle Kyle?" Kylie brought up her other sticking point.

"We'll figure it out," her father insisted. There was a note of finality in his tone.

The three of them attempted to go back to what they'd been doing—her parents were particularly valiant and stubborn about it—but Kylie was pretty sure it was all for show. A couple of times she caught her mom and dad with their heads together, but if their tight expressions meant anything, they never did come up with an alternate plausible solution.

Like she had for a week, Kylie tossed and turned all night long. She needed to align her thoughts in some way that would provide her with some answers, but she couldn't seem to come up with anything useful. One o'clock in the morning found her downstairs in her family's kitchen, steeping a cup of honey vanilla chamomile tea. She felt tired but restless as she stirred a spoon through the steaming hot liquid.

"Kylie," her mom's voice reached her from the doorway. Kylie jumped, startled. She, too, was barefoot and in her bathrobe. "Sorry, honey. Didn't mean to scare you. What are you doing up?"

"Couldn't sleep."

Her mom came up behind where Kylie was sitting at their kitchen island on a stool and hugged her. Kylie rested her head on her mom's shoulder. "What are we going to do, Mom?"

"Your father and I have discussed finding jobs elsewhere."

"But your heart and soul have been poured into this business. Both you and Daddy's. For as long as I can remember."

"That doesn't matter. This is just brick and mortar, machines and fabric. I can run an alterations business out of the house on a reduced scale, and your father has been going online to job sites all evening. We're going to do a workaround for this. Don't you worry."

After getting herself her own tea, her mom vanished back upstairs. But Kylie couldn't obey her edict of not worrying. Her parents were ready to upend their lives and everything they'd worked for over two solid decades to build for her. And for what? Because they were afraid of her going out a time or two with Tony Menotti?

Granted, he could be lying. He could be a snake in the grass. But what if he wasn't? What if he meant what he said and would seriously lower the amount taken from their profits as long as she agreed to spend a little time with him?

She continued to sip her tea, regarding her surroundings. She and her parents didn't have the fanciest home in the world, but it was theirs. It was cozy and in a good, low-crime area with a mix of nice neighbors of various ages, cultures, and backgrounds. They'd already gotten to know several of them. The lady across the street had even brought them over a homemade cake when they'd moved in.

Her father had been so proud when he'd found this house because as a two-story it was larger than their last home but cost the exact same price. She and her mom had had so much fun decorating it and putting their original and familiar belongings into the fresh new spaces. And her Uncle Kyle's nursing home was a ten-minute drive away. He needed them. They couldn't abandon him.

She couldn't allow her parents to give up the business they'd dreamed of running and had successfully been the owners of for years. That would mean that these terrible mafia members would win while her good, hard-working family would lose. Soundly.

Her thoughts went in vicious circles. What if she agreed to go out with Tony Menotti? What if she refused?

An hour later, Kylie stood rinsing out her cup. She commenced climbing the stairs back to her room, forgetting about the squeak of the seventh stair and causing the noise to reverberate loudly to her own ears. Luckily, the house remained silent except for the settling of its foundations and the ticking of clocks. Maybe her parents had found sleep after all.

Moving more carefully, she slipped into her room. Tugging off her robe, she slid into bed, pulling the covers around her as if the comfort of her blankets would be enough to convince her body to drift off. Then, miracle of miracles, slumber took her.

THE NEXT MORNING dawned with partly cloudy skies and higher temperatures than they'd experienced all year. It was eight-thirty, a half hour before they opened, and she was straightening supplies out front, pulling the ready orders to the beginning of the automated line, when Tony Menotti arrived at the door. He pushed on it to find it locked, then glanced down at their hours. She hurried over to him, put a finger to her lips in a shushing motion, then opened the door for him.

"This is very clandestine," he remarked with a mischievous grin. "I like it."

Dial down the flirty charm there, bucko.

The problem was that this man represented a powerful criminal organization who could basically do whatever they wanted. If they so desired, they could burn her parents' building to the ground. They could do all manner of foul things. It would be best to play their game for now. Kylie couldn't allow something horrible to happen to her parents. She'd sacrifice herself before she let that occur. She didn't see any other available options.

"How much of a reduction in price would a date with you buy my folks, Mr. Menotti?" Kylie spoke as if their conversation from the previous day was continuing without interruption.

"Tony, please," he said, tipping his face downwards and glancing through his lashes at her. Kylie couldn't help but notice that his eyes were the golden-brown color of butterscotch. They sparkled as he grinned at her.

Okay, okay, enough of that. *Focus*.

"Fine, then, Tony. First, thank you for giving us a night to sleep on it," she told him in a rushed whisper. She didn't want her parents discovering what she was up to.

"My pleasure, *bellisima*," he responded, also keeping his voice low.

"Next, I'm going to go out on a limb here and ask you to please not kill or maim me."

She realized the second she said it that those words might be ridiculously dangerous to say. But it was too late. They were already out there. Tony didn't seem to take offense, though, much to her surprise.

"That would hardly be good etiquette," he quipped. "Not only would it be rude, it'd be bad for business."

"You consider killing and maiming rude?"

"Yes. It's a nasty business and usually utterly unnecessary."

"Usually?"

"That's called a joke, *bellisima*. The last thing I would ever want to do is hurt you in any way. I like you. I'd like to get to know you better."

Kylie waved her hand between them in a dismissive gesture. She had as good a sense of humor as the next girl, but this wasn't something she wanted to joke about. "So, your family? Is all you people care about business? Is it the money you really want?"

"May I be frank?"

"Please."

"The money is why I'm here. Collecting it is my duty. But it's hardly the only thing worth having. Most of the best parts of life have nothing whatsoever to do with cold, hard cash."

Interesting. A philosophical mobster. Who knew? Still, she needed to negotiate with him somehow. It was time to put the bartering skills she'd learned in her Economic Trade class to the test.

"If I agree to go out with you, and that is an 'if,' how much of a reduction in price are we talking about?"

"How much would you like to ask for?" he volleyed back.

All righty, then. "One date, one hour long, for forty-five hundred off the price."

His grin widened. "You drive a hard bargain, Ms. Cormier. But then, so do I. How about ten dates, four hours long each, for five hundred off the price. Do all that within the month, and you'll owe exactly zero."

Kylie stared at him. "You'll let me trade it all the way down to nothing?"

His expression didn't change. "I don't see why not."

"Four dates, two hours long, twelve hundred fifty dollars off each."

He chuckled as if this were more entertaining than anything he'd ever done before. "Eight dates, three hours long, sixteen hundred dollars each."

"Five dates, an hour and a half long, one thousand each," she countered.

"Done," he said, appearing as pleased as if he'd just won the lottery.

"Seriously?" she asked a little noisily, forgetting herself.

"Yes. Now, we should set up an appropriate time."

Thinking quickly, which was much easier now that she'd actually slept, she suggested, "How about Friday afternoons at one o'clock? We could meet at the Stuffed Potato Kitchen—it's a restaurant over on the UNT campus where I go to school. We could start there next week."

On Fridays, she had an 11 AM lecture and then a 3 PM economics class. If she finagled her time just right, she should be able to squeeze him in for some lunch dates without her parents even being privy to them. This had the added benefit of taking place in broad daylight, too. A girl couldn't be too careful.

"Deal," he said, thrusting out his hand. She moved to shake it, but at the last moment, he raised it to his lips and kissed it. Then, he pulled away from the threshold, waved to her as he opened the door of his Escalade, and drove off, his vehicle vanishing from the lot.

CHAPTER SIX

TONY SAT IN YET ANOTHER BUSINESS DINNER, SPOOLING HIS fettuccini in his spoon endlessly without taking a bite. Their cook Vittorio had probably made his signature Alfredo sauce just as wonderful and cheesy as he always did, but Tony's mind wasn't on food. Nor had it been for the past week plus. His mind was on the time he'd be spending with a certain Kylie Cormier tomorrow.

Not that Tony hadn't dated previous to now. Far from it. While his schooling had been fairly isolated, Sandro had gone out of his way to take Tony out to more public venues to simply mingle. Tony could still remember the first time he'd gone to those nightclubs dressed in jeans and a button-down rolled up to his elbows. Women had gravitated to him, making socializing easy. Over the years, he'd wondered if they'd known which family he'd belonged to or not, then decided it didn't really matter. He'd had a good time and that was what counted.

Then, a few times a year, his mother had thrown these massive parties and had invited every elite in Dallas.

There had been local TV personalities, prominent professional fishermen, a couple of the Dallas Cowboys, college deans and professors, the presidents from high-end golf clubs, and, of course, any businessperson who ran in their circles. There were even people there in official capacities like some up-and-comers from the mayor's office and a smattering of law enforcement, people Tony now realized were most likely in his father's pocket.

He'd been conscious of others' perceptions of him. Back at those parties, Tony had played his violin on occasion, always to accolades he didn't know were sincere or not. But while some of those partygoers knew exactly who his father was and the role the Menottis had to play in the Dallas infrastructure, he suspected most had no idea of the real internal workings of his family. Until very recently, even *he* hadn't been privy to the internal workings of his family.

He glanced up at the wall over the fireplace and let his eyes linger on the painted portrait of his family from fifteen years ago. In it, his father stood tall and aloof at the back while his mother had been seated in a tufted antique chair. He and his brother stood on either side of her, each with a hand on her shoulder. He'd been seven at the time and Sandro twelve. Back then, his father had had no silver in his dark hair, nor had his mother, though her hair was much lighter, almost blonde. In the portrait, it looked as if it'd been made of spun caramel.

Feeling a pang in his chest, Tony tore his gaze away from the painting again, his eyes instead flitting to the end of the table opposite his father. The empty place where his mother had once sat. This had been back before their family dinners had become business meetings, back when they'd actually felt like real family instead of a handful of men consumed by nothing but work.

Tony missed the old days greatly. It'd been over a year since his mother had sat at this table, but it still felt like yesterday. It'd come as such a shock losing Elliana Menotti. One moment she'd been there, asking for more of his charcoal drawings and presiding over the family's social calendar. Then, in the next, she'd been gone. Taken away from them by a twist of fate. Unbidden, the mangled remains of the car his mother had been riding in burst into his memory.

As per Menotti family unwritten rules, it was a simple black BMW Series 5 sedan. His family still didn't know precisely what had caused the accident. It hadn't been the weather because there hadn't been a cloud in the sky that day. But whatever it had been, it resulted in the driver—a man named Bruno—losing control. The sedan had flipped over at least twice and had come to a halt against the concrete foundation of a nearby underpass. Both his beloved *mamma* and the driver had been killed immediately.

Dredging all these memories up again had caused Tony's chest to feel tight, so he set his fork and spoon down and gulped some ice water instead. Unfortunately, this didn't go unnoticed.

"What? Not hungry?" Pietro asked from two chairs down, his face set in a smart-alecky grin.

Tony didn't deign to answer him.

"You've barely touched your food. Or is it that you're, I don't know, distracted maybe?" Pietro went on, as Dante smirked between him.

"I'm fine," Tony spoke harshly, not knowing what they were up to but annoyed just the same. He had been distracted, but he didn't need to hear their ceaseless and inane chatter right now.

"You know who else is *fine*?" Dante piped up on the heels of his brother's gibes. He reminded Tony of an eager lapdog.

"Who might that be?" Pietro played along superciliously.

Tony scowled deeply, already knowing he wouldn't like this.

"Why, that sweet little Comer girl at the laundry—" Dante began, but Tony cut him off. Seizing his cousin's silky silver tie, he tightened down on the thing until it worked more like a noose than a spare piece of clothing.

"Measure your next words extremely carefully, *cugino*. Because the Ms. *Cormier* who works at her family's *dry cleaners* is off limits to you." Tony's words came out as a quiet but formidable snarl as he continued to apply pressure to his cousin's throat. Hisses and gasps escaped Dante as his complexion went from red to blue. He clawed at Tony's wrists to let him go, but Tony didn't release him, keen to illustrate his point.

"Antonio," his father called, and only then did he unwrap Dante's tie from around his hand and sit back in his seat. Sandro's eyes were stationed on the three of them, too.

"Yes, *Papà*?"

"What is going on?"

"Nothing of consequence, sir. A minor disagreement," Tony told him, keeping things vague. His cousins did not know of the deal he'd made with Kylie, nor did his father. And Tony planned to keep it that way. At least for now.

"See that it stays minor," the patriarch continued. "I don't appreciate scuffles interrupting family meals."

"Of course not, *Papà*."

"How is your foray into visiting our protected businesses going so far?" Viktor asked, and though his eyes remained on his chicken alfredo, Tony knew his ears were fully tuned in to whatever he reported.

"Well." He'd already detailed a brief account of what had happened that day with the Boccias. "We've detected no further infringements from the Boccias or anyone else since that initial standoff."

"No one should leave the estate unarmed," Sandro added in, standing as his father's second-in-command. Declaring rules to be followed that remained in line with the patriarch was the responsibility of any good heir. "And be doubly on the lookout as you do your rounds. If the Boccias plan to stir up trouble over a border dispute, we'll all need to be on our guard."

Tony and his cousins nodded dutifully, though Dante also had to rub at his throat. He seemed to have difficulty swallowing, but Tony wasn't about to apologize. He didn't like that he and Pietro kept referring to the Cormiers' daughter above and beyond any of the others they regularly visited. If he had to put Dante in his place again, Tony would be sure to do it away from the calculating gaze of his father, though. Viktor didn't appreciate disention in the ranks.

Besides, Tony had better things to think about. Tomorrow would be his first covert meeting with the beautiful Kylie, and he was anxious to see how it would play out. Would she honor the commitment? Or would she back out of it? Perhaps he shouldn't have agreed to such an unusual request, but it was too late now. He'd just have to see how it went.

The next afternoon found him at the little café, sitting outside enjoying the warm spring day. He watched the line that snaked out of the building and down the side-walk while he waited. The place was popular, that much was for certain. College-aged kids meandered everywhere, with only a few of them offering him a second glance.

He'd decided to go slightly more incognito today, driving a black Audi R8 coupe, and dressing down a bit by taking off his suit jacket and tie and rolling up the sleeves of his white button-down with his Armani slacks. This sort of suit was far fancier than even professors tended to wear and would stand out too much otherwise.

As he watched behind his tinted window, Kylie Cormier came into view. Her long, light brown hair glowed lighter in the sun, and she looked somewhat nervous as she adjusted the book bag she had slung over one shoulder. Swiftly, he tugged himself free of the driver's side door and casually sauntered over to her. He had nearly reached her before she caught sight of him, her face going a little pale. He felt a compulsion to remedy that.

"Ah, *bellisima*. How nice to see you here."

She squared her shoulders. "It is what we agreed to," her tone came off as frosty. Oh, well. He could work with that.

"Tell me about this place." He indicated the massive white letters on a red background behind her, spelling out The Stuffed Potato Kitchen.

"Well, it's good," she sputtered out, then checked herself. "All the other students rave about it."

"I don't care one whit about what other students say about it," he said, and she peered at him, wide-eyed. "I care what *you* say about it."

"I... it's my favorite place on campus. It might look a little kitschy," she lowered her voice for her next sentence. "But it reminds me of home. They have crawfish etouffee and blackened shrimp, and their barbecue is yummy, too. I'm only on campus long enough to eat here on Fridays, but when I have the extra money, this is where I come."

"I can't imagine a better recommendation."

They took their place in line. Typically, Menottis didn't wait in line, especially at five-star establishments, but this was hardly five-star. Still, he wanted to experience this. Not only because Kylie seemed comfortable here—in fact, the longer she talked about the place, the more comfortable she seemed—but also because he'd never been to college. The students traipsing about everywhere were barely younger than him. In another life, he might have been one of them.

Tony kept the conversation going by asking her questions about her classes, her professors, and anything else she wished to tell him. Once they retrieved their food and found a shaded bench to sit on not far away, their discussion flowed like river currents. Maybe because he found everything she said genuinely interesting, their lunch interaction went by even faster than he'd anticipated.

"I know it probably sounds boring, but I love economics. The professor for that class, Dr. Eby, is so laid-back and down to earth. He likes to talk what-if scenarios about economic systems and how they work. We've practically applied a set-up in the classroom where we're a village. We've worked with planned economies, market economies, and mixed economies. Each has its advantages and disadvantages. It's so fascinating to me," she said, her aqua blue eyes bright and animated, and on the rare occasions when she'd smiled at him, two dimples had popped out on either side of her lips.

Tony felt glad he'd nicknamed her at first sight. *Bellisima* was indeed appropriate for the likes of Kylie Cormier.

"I'm sorry," she apologized later after telling him about the rigors of accounting. "I'm just going on and on. You should stop me."

"And why would I want to do that?" he asked her, one side of his mouth quirking upwards.

"Because I've basically taken over. We've hardly discussed you at all." She went quiet then, as if realizing the reality of who he was.

"I've enjoyed hearing about your exploits." It was true. The enthusiasm she felt lit up her face from within as if there was simply far too much curiosity and intelligence to hold it all inside. He didn't think he'd ever encountered such a phenomenon before. Or such a person. Still, she had asked. "Well, my upbringing has been… somewhat different from yours."

A flash of hesitation—or was it apprehension—crossed her features then, like she felt fearful of what he might tell her.

She glanced down at her hands as she rubbed little circles over the fine wrist bone on her left with her right index finger. Was this a tell of hers? He wondered what it meant.

"How so?" Her voice was soft.

"Where you grew up in public school with lots of students, I grew up being tutored with quite limited social interactions. Other than my cousins and my older brother, I didn't mix much except with other adults."

"That explains it, then," she said, more to herself than to him.

"Explains what?"

"You just seem… I don't know. Older. I don't mean that in a bad way, but you come across as far more mature than most of the college boys I'm around all the time."

He furrowed his brows, not liking the sound of her being surrounded by "college boys." When he thought of that term, he imagined drunken frat boys who got up to all sorts of crude shenanigans both amongst themselves and with their coeds. "What are they like?"

She merely shrugged. "Mostly just juvenile. Their idea of a good time is often pranking each other or saying something tacky to the women I have classes with, especially the sorority crowd."

"Have they ever said something untoward to you?" He clenched his fists together behind his back. He would take care of the issue immediately if so.

"No. I kind of fly under the radar here, if you want to know the truth," she said, continuing to trace her wrist bone. Fly under the radar? With her bright smile, adorable dimples, and gorgeous aqua eyes, she shone like a beacon to him. "I'm not really interested in that type of guy anyway. They don't make the best of impressions."

He focused his gaze in on hers. "And what kind of impression am I making?"

CHAPTER SEVEN

WHAT KIND OF IMPRESSION WAS HE MAKING? TALK ABOUT being put on the spot. It was amazing how easy it was being with Tony Menotti. There was something calming about his presence that she couldn't put her finger on. Which, considering the man was a real-life mobster, shocked her. She needed to be careful. Kylie felt like she'd been letting her barriers down with him when what she should've been doing was reinforcing them.

She cleared her throat.

"A good one, all things considered," she answered, subtly talking a half-step further away from him. They'd been walking through the campus, and now they'd come up to the oblong shape of the new student center. The university had totally tricked out the grounds with freshly planted trees and lots of decorative landscaping, and she kept her eyes on these details, feeling like he might not let her get away with such a vague reply. Instead, he glanced up to the sloped roof above them with a thoughtful look on his face.

"All things considered," he echoed, sardonically. "Nice to know."

"I didn't mean to sound… um… insulting or anything." Great. Now, she'd just wrongfooted herself.

If he'd noticed the distance she'd created, he said nothing about it. Nor did he *do* anything about it. He merely continued to amble along beside her. She couldn't help but note that he wasn't exactly volunteering any information about himself. It bugged her since she'd blabbed so much about herself. Too much, probably.

"No offense taken. I imagine many people have far worse things to say about my *famiglia*."

Heat flooded her face. What had she been thinking agreeing to this date? She could do the wrong thing with a fleeting slip of the tongue and possibly cost her family more trouble than they were already in.

"Uh… so you were tutored," she attempted to save both face and the conversation. Now she felt as if she were treading on particularly thin eggshells.

"I was. In many subjects, though my main focus for most of those years was art and music."

She blinked at him, not expecting that answer. "Oh?"

He met her gaze with his, and again she was reminded of butterscotch candy. "You sound shocked."

"Oh, well…" He'd flustered her. What was she supposed to say now? *I didn't know big bad mafia men were so refined and cultured?*

He actually chuckled at her. "I am the second son, *bellisima*. That means that I was somewhat removed from the main dealings of my *famiglia*. My father concentrated the majority of his teachings on my brother, Sandro, and this enabled me to pursue more of what my mother wanted for me."

His face warmed as he spoke about his mother.

"What types of art and music did you study?"

"A great many of them. My education was quite extensive. But my favorites became charcoal drawings and playing the violin. My mother even located a Stradivarius for me to play during concerts she would throw in her social circles. It's a treasure, and I used to love playing it."

"Used to? You don't anymore?"

"I…" A flash of something crossed his face then, something sad, if she wasn't mistaken. "I haven't had the heart to play it since my mother's death. It was her favorite, you see."

"I'm sorry for your loss. When did she die?" Kylie watched as everything about him changed. His posture slumped perceptively, and his face fell as he averted his eyes.

"Last March. Car accident." His voice sounded tight. Pained. Whatever else Tony Menotti might be, he'd loved his mother. His anguish and grief were written all over him like neon signs.

Time to change the subject. "If we keep going, we'll run into the Law School. I'm not planning to be an attorney, but the fountain is very pretty. If we stand at just the right spot at just the right time of day, we might see some rainbows coming off it."

He looked her in the face then, his eyes soft with gratitude. "By all means, lead on, *bellisima*."

"May I ask you about something?" she asked as she directed their steps on the correct trajectory.

"Of course."

"What does *bellisima* mean?"

"Very beautiful," he responded boldly, observing her head-on. "It was the first thing I thought when I laid eyes on you."

"Is that why you offered me this deal?" She felt her cheeks heating again. Kylie hadn't meant for those words to fly out of her, but now that they were out there, she was dying to know the answer.

"In part," he said, mysteriously. Saying nothing else on the matter.

When they made it over to the Law School, they meandered along the perimeter of the fountain outside its entrance.

"I'm not sure if we'll be able to see it at this point in the afternoon." Kylie traipsed along, leaning over to observe the fountain from various directions as they went. "Maybe if we go to this side…" Again, Tony allowed her to show him the way. After making two full circuits with no luck, she threw her hands up. "Must be the wrong time of day."

She flopped down on the raised concrete side, disappointed, when that angle provided the right vantage. The rainbow was faint but there. All seven colors—red, orange, yellow, green, blue, indigo, and violet—present.

The heat of the day had been increasing to hot levels, but there under a gentle Texas breeze, the wind carrying a subtle amount of spray over to them, it felt cool and comfortable. Or again, maybe that was her lunch date. Kylie had expected him to look out of place as he sat beside her on her college campus, but he didn't. Despite his more formal dress, if he switched his dress pants for jeans and threw a backpack over his shoulder, he would've fit right in. Even if he was more handsome—okay, considerably more handsome—than much of the male student body.

They sat there together in companionable silence for a few minutes before he broke it. "Say something else."

"Pardon?"

"Say something else. Anything."

"I don't catch your meaning," she said, perplexed.

"You have a lovely accent, *bellisima*. I delight in listening to it. After the end of this date, I'll be calling you not only because that is good etiquette and appropriate to our situation, but also so I can hear your unique pronunciation."

She knew she and her parents had a bit of an accent compared to the others in this area. Having been brought up in New Orleans had definitely left its mark on her speech patterns. She'd once been targeted by a rather mean-spirited girl for it when she had rudely asked, "Why are you talking like that?"

Raising her head high, Kylie had responded with, "I'm proud of my Louisiana heritage." The girl had scoffed, sticking her nose in the air as she traipsed off, her snooty group of friends following suit. Despite herself, it'd made Kylie feel like a round peg trying unsuccessfully to slot itself into a square hole.

Yet, just like that, Tony Menotti had made her feel redeemed. Though he carried almost no accent himself, other than when he spoke Italian, his speech patterns tended to be way more formal than hers or anyone else's she knew. But like him, she found that she liked it. His voice was melodic to listen to. Even soothing.

"Right back at you," she said, the corners of her mouth tugging upwards despite herself. She liked being with him, which was absurd. She was supposed to be doing this because she'd brokered a deal with him to lower her family's "payments," not because she wanted to be with him. She had to keep her family at the center of this, not her strange compulsion to get to know him. She shouldn't be *getting to know him* at all. That wasn't the point.

The Menottis were the cause of her family's struggles, and Tony himself was the main bad guy in this scenario. She'd do well to remember that. If he and his associates weren't so resolved to bleed their business coffers dry, she wouldn't be in this position in the first place. She needed to keep her distance from him, both metaphorically and literally.

Annoyed with herself, she turned her tone to something much colder. She pulled out her phone and noted the time, not bothering to be subtle about it. "Look, I need to get back to class soon. It's been an hour and a half, which should meet the qualifications we outlined." She could be formal, too, when necessary.

He regarded her, obviously taking in this switch in her attitude as his slight grin melted right off his overly attractive features. Why did he have to be so attractive, anyway? It diverted her from her true goals. Straightening, he nodded at her just as formally. "It has been an honor and a privilege spending time with you today, *bellisima*. Shall we meet again at the same time next Friday?"

"That will be fine," she said stiffly.

"In the same location by the Stuffed Potato?"

It sounded almost funny hearing his cultivated—and yes, delicious—voice say the words, "Stuffed Potato."

"That works for me."

"Would you like me to accompany you to this class?"

"*No*," she gusted out a little too quickly. She felt bad, so she softened her tone by a degree or two. "No, that won't be necessary. Thank you."

He didn't question anything further; instead, he clutched at her hand, kissing the back of it like he had when they'd made their agreement back in the doorway of her family's business. "Until then, *bellisima*." And without another word, he made an about-face and stalked with purpose across the Law School's brick walkway.

CHAPTER EIGHT

THAT EVENING, TONY RETURNED TO HIS *FAMIGLIA'S* ESTATE IN an edgy state. As well as the date with Kylie Cormier had gone initially, things had become rather disheartening near the end. It'd happened without warning, too, like a tornado out of a clear, blue sky. It seemed as if she had flipped something off inside of her, and the warm, blushing young woman he'd had such a great time with during their lunch and subsequent walk morphed into someone else. Someone with a much chillier disposition.

It might not have bothered him so much had he known the reason why.

He'd reviewed everything they'd spoken of about a dozen times in his head, picking it apart like notes in a musical composition, but he couldn't identify the why of it. What had he done? He'd been so careful to not divulge much about how his *famiglia* handled their affairs, yet she'd acted as if someone had sat her down to see their extensive list of offenses in black and white. He didn't want to lie to her—at least not unless it was through omission—but he couldn't defend against evidence he didn't know about.

Why had everything turned on a dime?

At last, after brooding about this for a whole evening, he comprehended that worrying wasn't a resourceful use of his time. What he and Kylie had was an arrangement, nothing more. Yes, he felt attracted to her, but it wasn't as if that could ever become more. He'd be unlikely to get the chance to pursue her in earnest, anyway. If he wanted to impress his father, he'd need to spend most of his energy and efforts meeting those ends.

After pulling cash out of the billion-dollar trust fund he shared with Sandro, he set it aside to make the Cormiers' payment at the end of the month.

At some point, he and Kylie would need to add a cut-off time in order to have five entries before the last day of May, but he'd known today wasn't the day to discuss it. Kylie had made that clear, and he was tired of worrying about it.

The important thing in all of this was that his father discovered that he was worth investing time in, that he could do the job Viktor had assigned him. He'd help Kylie —though why he wanted to, he wasn't that certain of at the moment—and meet his father's requirements at the same time. He liked and appreciated the idea of killing two birds with one stone. It not only made sense, it would be an efficient way to conduct business.

He could admit to being attracted to Kylie, that wasn't a problem. But whether or not pursuing extra time with her would be worth it, he couldn't tell. He didn't want to give up on her, though. At least, not yet. If she became more trouble than she was worth, he'd consider letting her go then but not before. Things with her might be up in the air for now, but he wasn't ready to make a final decision where she was concerned.

Plus, there was a thrill to playing both sides against the middle like he was. He'd never attempted something like this, and though it was a bit harrowing, he also liked the adrenaline rush it offered him. There was no denying that he was playing a dangerous game sneaking around like this, but he knew he could easily save face if need be. This early on, he could simply renege on everything and demand the Cormiers pay whether they wanted to or not.

He did like being the nice guy in Kylie's eyes, though.

Putting the portion of cash in his own personal lockbox he kept in a special hidden compartment he'd sawed into the back of his closet, he set the money aside. If things went according to plan, Kylie would continue to date him, and he'd continue to pay in place of her parents. He hoped by the time they'd had their five dates she'd agree that this was an amenable solution to her problem. He could keep getting to know her and determine how he wanted things to proceed from there.

Even if she had all but rebuffed him earlier.

Feeling too stuck inside his own head, he changed into athletic attire and went for a jog along the grounds of the Menotti estate. If that wasn't enough, he'd go work out in his *famiglia's* home gym. He felt almost fidgety and didn't enjoy having the extra energy pent up in his system. What started out as a jog became a hard sprint as he worked to rid himself of whatever this underlying tension was that wouldn't leave him alone.

He passed the bald cypress trees planted at the back of their property, their conical shapes rising into the sultry air. He careened by the long, paved patio and Olympic-sized pool that they had used mainly to entertain other people during his mother's parties. And he raced beyond the outskirts of the biggest building on their estate, the main house where his father, his mother, his brother, and Tony himself each had their own separate wings.

As the sun lowered along the horizon, it cast the white marble façade at the front of his home into shades of oranges and reds. Unlike almost everything else they owned, including their attire, rather than the dark colors of formal elegance, their house honored their Italian heritage by paying homage to Roman architecture. The Corinthian columns that adorned the Colosseum also adorned their estate, standing as a testament to a past Tony scarcely felt a connection to. Still, home was home.

After running full out around the perimeter of the estate, barely noticing the bland, gray high-security wall he ran next to, he still felt restless. Deciding that his muscles needed more resistance than the humid Dallas atmosphere could offer him, he paused to unlock then push through the thick steel double doors at the front of the massive house, preparing to do a circuit of weightlifting in his *famiglia's* sizable home gym.

He'd just started pumping some free weights with his left arm when his brother came in. "*Fratello*, did you withdraw some money from the trust? I received a notification from the banking app."

Tony hadn't realized such a notification would be triggered by his actions.

"I did." Tony wasn't going to deny it. Not to Sandro. When his brother raised his eyebrows, waiting for an explanation, Tony shrugged. "Let's just say I have a project I'm working on."

"Perhaps it would be better if I don't know the specifics," Sandro said, shaking his head.

"Perhaps. Not you and even more so not *Papà*."

He sighed, joining Tony in lifting weights. Sitting on the bench beside him, he added, "Maybe I should forego mentioning that whatever game you're playing, it's a risky one."

"That would be appreciated."

"Fine. So, you've gotten involved in the dirty part of the business against my advice. How's it going?"

"I'm making it work. The most irritating part of it is dealing more directly with Pietro and Dante. I've always known they could be exasperating but having them in such close quarters with me daily only highlights the fact."

"Our *cuginos* are a handful. They've been that way since they were children and haven't improved with age. What can I say, Antonio? You asked for it."

"Perhaps," he said again.

"I know what you're doing, you know," Sandro said, switching arms. A light line of perspiration gathered along his ebony hairline.

"Is that so?"

"Yes. You want more than our father's attention and approval." Tony didn't respond, choosing to continue pumping iron instead. "You realize he is no replacement for *Mamma*, don't you? He's not capable of offering her tender loving care."

A jab of fury ignited along Tony's spine. His brother's accusation hit far too close to his father's dismissal of him at their recent dinner. "I am not a boy and don't *need* tender loving care. Not from him or anyone else. Besides, that's fine for you to say. You already have *Papà's* favor."

"I don't have his favor." Sandro scowled at him pointedly. "What I have is first-born status. That's all. I didn't ask for any of this. To be the heir or to have to take on the responsibility of his mantle someday. But that responsibility *is* mine, and I must live up to it to secure our *famiglia's* legacy. I have to take this all seriously."

"Are you saying I'm not taking my own role seriously?"

"No, I'm not. Quite the opposite. You're taking it far too seriously." Sandro released a noisy exhale, tossing down the metal twenty-pound weight with a raucous clang on the rack with more force than was needed. "All I'm saying is that you're better than this life. I didn't have a choice in who I had to be, but you do. It's still not too late to back out. It's still not too late to keep from wasting your time pursuing a criminal lifestyle."

"You don't want me to succeed," Tony accused his brother.

"I don't want you to *die*," Sandro pitched back with a raised voice, making Tony take a step back. His brother had customarily been the most level-headed of the two of them, so this rare fit of temper showed just how invested in this he was. "Haven't we had enough of that in our *famiglia*?"

That statement halted Tony in his tracks. He could hear the sorrow in his brother's voice, could see it etched in each one of his features. "If something happens to you, *fratello*," Sandro went on, "I don't know what I'll do."

"Nothing is going to happen to me." Tony's objection came out without any intensity or heat as he laid a hand on Sandro's shoulder. He didn't want to battle his beloved older brother on this. He just wanted to be included amongst the *famiglia* he had left. "The last thing I want is to die or to watch any of my other loved ones die. But I know I can be of help. I can have your backs. There is safety in numbers, right? So, the more numbers we have, the safer all of us will be."

Tony never said the name Boccias, but the implication of their rivalry with them hung like a heavy yoke between them. Seeing the manner in which they conducted themselves up close and personal for the first time at the Cormiers' establishment had shed some light on what to expect from them in the future.

Sandro smiled at him, but there was no joy or humor in it. If anything, it appeared resigned. "Numbers mean exceedingly little when an unseen sniper has the barrel of his long-range rifle aimed at the back of your head. I do appreciate you wanting to support us, though, I do. And since this is so important to you, I'll be certain to support you."

"You always have," Tony pointed out. The only person to praise Tony for his art and music as much as his dear *mamma* had been Alessandro.

Like he was a chubby-faced toddler, his older brother ruffled his hair, leaving it a spiky mess. "And I always will."

CHAPTER NINE

TONY: I WOULD LIKE TO MEET YOU BY THE LAW SCHOOL **fountain for our next date.**

Kylie glared down at the text she'd received, the muscles in her upper back, neck, and shoulders tensing automatically. Their next date would begin in fifteen minutes, which meant she'd need to backtrack away from the Stuffed Potato and hoof it over to the Law School as fast as she could instead. The man could have at least given her more notice. She felt aggravated, and not just because he'd altered their plans with no warning.

She felt aggravated because their first date—which technically shouldn't have been considered a date at all—had gone far too well. She'd actually enjoyed herself, if she was honest, and it freaked her out. Enjoying herself hadn't been the plan. Tony Menotti wasn't some normal college guy she could hang out with and get to know. He was a full-fledged criminal whose family was holding the same thing as a bounty over her head. She shouldn't have had a good time, and it infuriated her to realize that she had.

So, she decided that this time, she wouldn't let him in. Not at all. She couldn't trust him as far as she could throw him, and that was reason enough. She'd be polite in a detached manner, but that was all she was willing to give him. That was all she could afford. This would be about fulfilling her obligation to him according to the terms they'd agreed upon and nothing else. She must remember that.

When he pulled up in his sleek, black Audi sportscar, she slid into his leather passenger seat without fanfare. Being in such close quarters meant she immediately registered his cologne, which was something light and spicy in the best of ways. But she didn't need to know how this man smelled. Today would be all about keeping things at surface level only.

"Hello, *bellisima*. I trust you're having a pleasant day."

See, that was part of the problem. He shouldn't be calling her very beautiful in Italian. It made them sound like something they weren't, something they'd never ever be.

"I'm not sure how I feel about you calling me that," she said, keeping her eyes forward so that they stared out his windshield.

"Why not, if I may be so bold to ask?"

"It's…" *I like it too much.* "Too informal. Too personal. And you and I don't know each other, not really."

He paused, scrutinizing her, his hands on his steering wheel while he remained parked on the side of the road. The fountain splashed nearby and so did the voices of the other students. They had no idea what Tony Menotti truly was, what he—or most certainly his organized crime family—was actually after.

"Tell you what. Let's go through with our date today, and if you still feel uncomfortable with my nickname for you, I'll never refer to you that way again. Will that work?" he asked, one side of his mouth quirking upwards. He always seemed so sure of himself. Too sure.

"I suppose."

"Very well."

He turned away, nudging his accelerator as he drove through the campus. She watched all the familiar sights going by, wondering if he had a plan for where he'd be taking her, but then, he left the UNT grounds entirely.

She twisted in her seat to narrow her eyes at him. "Where are we going? Where are you taking me?" she demanded in a voice too high for its own good.

"Home," he said simply, and her heart stuttered. Why in the world would he take her home with him? It couldn't be for any good or upstanding reason. What if once he brought her there, he'd take her prisoner? Or sell her? Or even murder her? Wasn't that what the mafia was most known for?

"This is outside the parameters of our deal," she objected.

He shook his head. "No, I don't believe so. I'll need to have you back to your university in time for your next class, but you never limited me on where I could take you."

Kylie opened her mouth only to shut it again. He was right. She thought she'd been more careful than this, but she hadn't been. The only real thing she'd had in mind while negotiating with him was helping her parents either lessen or not incur such a vast debt. She hadn't gotten overly detailed beyond that. Fearful now, she tried to think of some way to talk him out of this as he drove a short distance away and up to an eight-foot-high iron gate.

Tony rolled down his window, plugged in a multi-numeric code, then said, "Hello, Federico. It's me."

"Master Antonio. Welcome," came a voice which crackled through the intercom, as a small motor sounded, opening the heavy metal gate.

Tony slowly navigated down a long, labyrinthine road better paved than any local street Kylie had seen until he approached a massive structure. Out front, two half-walls of limestone bookended an entry into a circle drive. At its center stood a copper fountain depicting what Kylie believed must be the Roman god Neptune, his three-pronged trident at his side for all to see.

Eclipsing that fountain, however, was a colossal three-story building that looked like a house on steroids. Everything about the place was grander than anything she'd ever seen in person before, with its columns along the front, its dome-shaped dormers, and its two balconies coming off two of the second-floor patios.

The place looked even more artfully landscaped than her college did with its carefully clipped shrubbery reaching in swirls toward the sky and its huge floor-to-ceiling windows across the façade. Two wide doors in a slate gray that matched the roofing shingles appeared behind the columns, their heavy, hammered hardware reminding Kylie of something she might expect to see on a medieval castle. If she'd ever imagined any building matching the definition of a mansion, this would have to be it.

"Home sweet home," Tony muttered as he stopped right in front of those doors. Astonishingly, they were unlocked as he escorted her inside.

The inside was even more jaw-dropping than the outside had been. The limestone had been replaced with white marble walls that opened up into an atrium that stretched upwards and encompassed all three of those stories. Overhead gleamed a massive crystal chandelier that made her think of *Beauty and the Beast*. Before them lay enough furniture for at least twenty people to comfortably sit in, and on either side of this expansive room were sweeping matching staircases that curved upwards into arches that led to the upper floors.

Awed despite herself, Kylie gasped. "You live here?"

Tony glanced down at his shoes briefly as if feeling humble. It wasn't the most natural of looks on him. "All my life."

"Why did you bring me to this place, Tony?"

He wrinkled his forehead. "Because I surmised at the end of our last date that you weren't all that at ease. I thought letting you get to know who I am might help."

Now it was she who wrinkled her forehead. "You want to let me get to know you?"

"Isn't that the purpose of dating?"

"But these aren't..." she trailed off. These weren't real dates, but it might be foolish of her to say such a thing out loud. If he thought they were, she'd need to placate him somehow. She needed him to hold up his end of this odd bargain they'd made. "All right. Other than how over-the-top luxurious your digs are, what did you want to show me?"

"Come," he said, reaching out an arm to her. This felt like a test to her, one she didn't dare fail.

She allowed him to lace his fingers with hers, hoping against hope that she wouldn't regret letting him lead her. He tugged her through the atrium and back deeper into the house. The further they went, the more impressed she felt by the extreme scale of the place against her will. They traversed a hallway filled with art pieces she'd only ever seen in art books, then continued through to a dining room with a wall-eating brick fireplace.

"It's right through here," he encouraged her, his face lit up like a little boy's. What was he up to? When he pushed through a sliding door, she was met with a glimmering stainless-steel kitchen nicer than she imagined most restaurants had. There was a professional-looking chef's stove with a double oven. A wide granite countertop wrapped all the way around, and in the middle sat an island with its own separate sink. "I admit I had to cheat a bit for the sake of time," he said as he opened the single biggest refrigerator Kylie had seen in her life. "I browned the meat mixture ahead of time."

Baffled, she stationed herself in one of the four cushioned barstools that lined one side of the island. "I don't understand."

"I'm making you lunch, *bellisima*. Or Kylie, if that's what you prefer."

She watched dumbfounded as he removed two metal bowls covered over with plastic wrap, packages of shredded mozzarella, cottage cheese, and something leafy she thought might be fresh herbs from the fridge, and placed them next to him on the counter. Then, he opened the cupboard door on what appeared to be a pantry—granted, it could probably feed the population of a third-world country—and retrieved two cans of tomato sauce.

"My *mamma*, God rest her soul, would strangle me if she knew I wasn't making the pasta fresh, but again…" He tapped on his watch, which Kylie suspected was a genuine Rolex.

Retrieving a long Pyrex cake dish, he opened one of the cans of tomato sauce and dumped half of it in the bottom. He washed his hands at the island sink, then, peeling back the plastic wrap from one of the metal bowls, he began laying some long noodles on top of the sauce.

"I know it looks messy," he said, grinning over at her. His features had been utterly transformed from the man who'd stormed into her parents' business. This person was much more boyish, much more eager. Much more *human*. "But just digging in with your bare hands is what makes it taste so good."

"What are you making?"

"Lasagna. It's *Mamma's* recipe passed down from her grandmamma. I guarantee that you'll like it." He continued layering in all the various ingredients until they filled the pan completely. Only as he sprinkled mozzarella over the entire concoction did he say, almost to himself, "I haven't made it since she passed."

His expression became much more somber after that, and Kylie stayed silent. She didn't know what to say.

Tony finished putting everything together and slid the whole thing into one of the ovens, setting the timer on the stove. When he glanced up, his face brightened again. "This should only take twenty minutes or so. Would you watch a show with me?"

She shrugged. "Sure." Why not? She just hoped it wouldn't be something super violent.

Still, she'd anticipated him putting on something like *Narcos* or *The Sopranos*, but that wasn't what he did. He moved open two wooden doors that matched the white of the rest of the cupboards, then started the Hulu streaming app. When he began an episode of *The Golden Girls*, she thought he was joking until he laughed out loud when Betty White commenced to go on and on about growing up in St. Olaf.

"You watch *The Golden Girls*?" she asked incredulously, half laughing herself. She guessed she really shouldn't saddle the guy with a stereotype, especially when he was as flesh and blood as she was.

"All the time. I used to watch with..." his words drifted into nothing as he kept his eyes on the television screen. It didn't take a genius to connect the dots, though. He used to watch it with his mother, someone he obviously still mourned.

The silence dragged on until Kylie volunteered some of her own information. "I used to watch with my grandma."

His golden brown eyes flicked in her direction. "Is she still alive?"

"No. She died when I was fifteen. She was an ornery and opinionated woman who loved to start arguments at every family get-together. She was a proud Cajun who spoke French I could never understand half the time. She was my mom's mom and got on her nerves like it was a sport. My dad went out of his way to avoid her."

"Sounds like a delightful lady," Tony offered with a smirk, his tone tongue in cheek.

"She was a pain in the heinie, no doubt, but I still miss her every single day."

CHAPTER TEN

THERE WAS REAL SORROW AND LOVE IN KYLIE'S VOICE AS SHE spoke of her grandmother. Tony understood. He could barely tolerate Pietro and Dante, but he did because they were his *famiglia*. And standing by one's *famiglia* was part and parcel of belonging. It was why Viktor had never discussed business around his wife. It was why his mother had stayed with his father even though Tony suspected she knew more about his doings than she ever let on.

The bonds of love and of blood were not meant to be broken.

This line of thought could easily take him down a path he'd rather not go on, so he decided to lighten the subject. "Who was her favorite *Golden Girls* character?"

"Sophia, of course. Though Rose will always be it for me. She might've been scatter-brained, but she was also sweet and, to me, the funniest one on there." Tony liked watching Kylie's eyes sparkle as she spoke about this topic and felt glad that he'd switched lanes. "You?"

"Oh, I love all of them."

"Nuh-uh," she wagged her finger at him. "That doesn't count. You can't say all of the above when you're supposed to pick only one."

"You know, you're quite opinionated yourself," he observed, smiling at her.

"Duh. I inherited it, fair and square. Now, choose." She sounded so bossy he almost snorted.

"Fine. I choose Bea Arthur's character, Dorothy. She was tough and no-nonsense. I liked her take-no-prisoners approach to life."

"Fair enough," she said, as if she'd proclaimed his answer as barely passing muster, just as the timer on the stove dinged.

"Lasagna time," he announced, and rapidly plated the food.

Pouring them both some Coke, he sat beside her, enjoying how cozy this felt. She seemed to have relaxed around him again, like she had in his car last week, and he didn't want to disturb the friendly rhythm of chatter they had going. He could get used to this, sharing meals with a bright and beautiful woman like Kylie. She fascinated him, and now that she had let her defenses down, he found himself feeling something toward her he didn't know how to describe. It was warm and buoyant. Something he'd like to feel as often as possible.

They were halfway through their second episode and almost finished with their food when he heard a sound that made him frown. The front doors had opened and shut, and footsteps echoed through the atrium loudly enough that he could hear whoever it was approaching the dining room. Frustrated, he ran through his options.

The reason he'd brought Kylie here today was because he should've had the place to himself other than their security personnel. They had a housekeeper who came once a week, but her staff wouldn't be in until tomorrow. His father was supposed to be across town playing a poker game, his cousins should be out doing rounds, and his brother typically spent every Friday practicing out at their privately owned shooting range two blocks away.

Yet it was Sandro who appeared from the dining room, already speaking as he pushed through the door. *"Fratello,* is that you?" He came to a halt with his eyebrows raised sky high the moment he spotted Kylie.

Tony hated to be taken unawares, but if anyone had to show up unexpectedly, his brother was the least problematic out of every other possibility. "Kylie Cormier, let me introduce my brother, Alessandro Menotti."

"How nice to meet you, Kylie," Sandro said, his tone cordial but with a tentative note to it. He wanted to know why she was here, that much was clear. In fact, his brother's eyes were full to the brim with questions. Better to nip this in the bud.

"If you'll excuse me for just one moment, Kylie. Please feel free to have as much lasagna as you'd like." Tony did an about-face and went back into the dining room, knowing his brother would follow.

"Care to explain?" Sandro whispered in a brisk tone, and irritated, Tony snapped.

"No one was supposed to be home right now."

"Well, I am home."

"That's stating the obvious."

"Antonio, I don't care about who you date, what I care about is why the daughter of one of the property owners who pays us protection money is sitting in our kitchen."

"How do you know who she is?" Tony asked him. He hadn't anticipated Sandro being privy to this information.

"It's my job to know all the goings-on in our *famiglia*, especially in regard to our business dealings. I make it a point to know. Now, tell me what you're doing with her."

"We made an arrangement. Her family can't afford to make the payments, so I told her I'd lower the amount if she went out with me."

Sandro scrunched up his face like an infant getting ready to let loose a scream. "Are you insane? The amount of protection money paid to us is set by the patriarch. It's not up for debate or bartering."

"I know that. That's why I'm covering it."

"That's why there are withdrawals from our account?" Sandro asked in blatant disbelief.

"There's a billion dollars plus in that account, *fratello*. This won't even make a dent in it."

"That's not the point. The point is that you're playing with fire with this girl. If our father finds out what you're up to, and that you've done all this behind his back, not only will he not trust you to transact any more business in his name, he'll punish you. Severely."

Sandro's words hung heavy in the air between them, and even though Tony could still hear the sounds of the sitcom he'd left playing in the kitchen, it didn't take away from the gravity of the moment.

"Are you going to tell him?" he asked his older brother, his chest going cold at the thought.

Sandro glowered at him. Rather than providing him with an answer, he began to stalk back and forth across the dining room carpet like a caged beast. Good thing the carpet was so thick and plush it muffled the sound. Through some miracle of restraint, they'd both managed to keep their voices down.

"No. No, I'm not. I won't rat out my little brother, not even to our father. But Antonio, you're balancing this on the fine edge of a razor blade. What I don't get is why you did this at such a crucial time. I thought you were attempting to impress the patriarch, not throw him onto the warpath."

"I…" he didn't finish his thought.

Tony knew Sandro was right, and while he'd recognized all along that he was taking a risk, the sheer scale of that risk hadn't really impacted him until now. If Viktor found out about what he was doing for Kylie, he could lose everything. His father's respect. His place in the organization. The patriarch might even disown him, ending any chance he may have had to grow closer to him as a parent.

Tony could end this. He could take Kylie back to school and tell her that he was breaking their deal. He could. Perhaps, he even should. But he didn't want to. The truth was he enjoyed Kylie Cormier's company. And not just as a distraction. He felt like something was there between them. Something that if he didn't take this chance to explore, he'd never forgive himself.

"I like her," he admitted finally.

Sandro stopped pacing and put his head in his hands. "*Fratello...*"

"No, Alessandro. I *like* her. And I'll figure this out. I promise."

His big brother regarded him with pursed lips and a deep line furrowed between his eyes. "You must be more cautious, then. Having her here... What if it'd been *Papà* who'd come home instead of me?"

"I agree," Tony said, nodding. "I won't be so negligent going forward."

"See that you aren't," Sandro told him, but though his words might've been harsh, the way he'd delivered them was anything but. He'd sounded concerned and anxious, not angry.

Tony's gaze stayed on his brother as he departed, probably heading up to his rooms. He'd turned to go back to the kitchen when he found Kylie standing there at the threshold. How long had she been standing there? Had she seen him and his brother arguing? Had she overheard their discussion?

"Is everything all right, Tony?"

"Why? Were our voices too loud?" he asked, waiting for her response.

"No, not at all. I couldn't even hear you. It's just that there's all this tension in the air that wasn't there before."

"Having you over might not have been the best idea," he confessed candidly. Might as well get it out there. "Have you finished your lunch?"

"Yes."

"Then, we should probably go."

"Yeah. Okay. My next class is in forty-five minutes."

He followed her back into the kitchen where she began to pick up her dishes. "No, I'll take care of that. Follow me."

Without question, she did as he asked, trailing after him as he guided her back through his home. Once they were safely back inside his Audi, he put his vehicle in gear and drove off the Menotti estate. Only after they'd left it far enough behind to be out of visual range did she speak.

"Your brother didn't like me being in your home."

"That's not quite accurate. The truth is, I didn't get permission from our patriarch to make this bargain with you. Sandro is worried that if my father were to find out, he would be upset with me."

"How upset?"

"Suffice it to say, more upset than your parents would ever be with you. He's a hard man, my *papà*. He's never been one to suffer fools, and since *Mamma's* death, he's only gotten fiercer about how he runs his house and our *famiglia*. Harsher. Crueler. I should've thought about that before bringing you over. I don't want you mixed up in any... unpleasantness."

Things became so quiet within the confines of his Audi he could've heard a pin drop. At last, she spoke up again.

"I want to thank you for putting yourself at risk to help my family."

"I'm not going to lie to you. I know that paying us money to keep you safe is not exactly lawful or even ethical, for that matter. But given the location of your parents' business, it is the lesser of two evils. Also, I can't claim that I made this deal with you for purely altruistic purposes. I am attracted to you, Kylie, and I feel like we get along well together. Dating you wasn't just a negotiation tactic for me. I really would like to see if this works."

He swallowed after saying his piece. He hadn't thought he'd be laying all his cards out on the table like this. But perhaps it was better this way. Even though he worked as a member of the mafia, he could be honest about this. They could never have anything real if he wasn't up front about everything anyway. Besides, Kylie deserved to know the truth.

She seemed lost in thought as he drove her back and didn't do much other than peer out her window. But as he stopped outside his customary spot beside the Law School fountain, she unbuckled her seatbelt, leaned over, and kissed him on the cheek.

"I've decided I don't mind you calling me *bellisima,* after all. Same time, same place, next week?"

His smile whisked across his face so rapidly that his face twinged. "Absolutely."

CHAPTER ELEVEN

DESPITE IT BEING SUMMER, KYLIE STILL WOKE JUST AFTER dawn. This came from years and years of getting up early to help her parents with the store. She still remembered being eleven and doing her homework at the counter— some things never change—when her father had asked her to get the tall extension hook they used to retrieve a customer's order. And because it'd been so busy that day, she done this for three hours straight.

Her mother had walked into the midst of all this productivity and kidded with those still waiting, "Do you think we should pay her? Our Kylie's a pretty decent employee."

There'd been a chorus of yeses and chuckles and quips. But the ironic thing was that Kylie had *yearned* to help. It'd always bothered her to stand by and watch her parents struggle to keep up with the demand, so pitching in didn't only feel good, it felt right. And over her preteen and early teenage years, she'd gradually become a part of the crew. At fourteen, when it became legal for them to legitimately put her on the payroll, they'd given her ten hours a week on the weekends.

From there, her hours grew to the point that by the time she was eighteen and a high school graduate, she worked full-time hours more often than not. When the few friends she had complained that she was never available, she'd simply told them that her family needed her. That may have been why other than her best friend, Shelley, nearly all of those friends eventually abandoned her.

That was one of the many things she and Tony had in common. He understood her devotion to family because he was just as devoted to his. She sat up, lost in a memory of them laughing about an episode of *Golden Girls* where Dorothy had hired a personal trainer. His butterscotch eyes had glimmered as his entire visage had lifted with amusement.

"Is that the one where she asks about leg warmers?" he asked, smiling his flawlessly white smile.

"Yep." Kylie grinned at both the image of the show in her head and at Tony's boyish enthusiasm. In moments like these, she forgot his mafia background altogether.

"And the trainer asks Dorothy how she keeps her thighs warm now?"

Nodding wildly, Kylie answered, "Yeah, and Dorothy says, 'Friction!'"

They both said "Friction" in unison, then burst out in crazy, no-holds-barred laughter. She fell into him and he caught her, hugging her to him as they'd sat beneath the shady gazebo at the heart of Dragon Park Gardens. The place was a private little plot of land full of unique sculptures and lots of trees and greenery. Many of the sculptures were of the more fantastic variety, including griffons, winged cherubs, and of course, dragons. Since the owners of the park were friends of Tony's art tutor, they always gave him free access any time of the night or day.

He and Kylie hung out there often. It'd become their own special getaway. A couple of months ago, she and Tony had given up the pretense of her going with him on dates as "payment" and now, they were simply dating. She didn't know whatever became of the mandate for her parents to pay the Menottis to protect them. After their first few dates back in May, Tony had stopped mentioning money at all. But no mafia members came to their door ever again, and that was what mattered most to Kylie.

Also, getting to know Tony over the past few months had been one happy surprise after another. Not only did the two of them have a similar sense of humor, they also looked at life much the same way. On paper, they might seem to be a nightmare of epic proportions. The mafia son and the devoted daughter and accounting student? Talk about incompatible. But in reality, that wasn't the case at all.

When they spent time together, Tony was thoughtful, creative, and solicitous of her. After she begged for him to bring some of his charcoal artwork to show her, he finally gave in and did so, blowing her away.

"Tony, these are so good. I mean, I'm no expert or anything, but if you framed these, they could be show-cased in a gallery somewhere."

He'd averted his eyes, all shy bashfulness all of a sudden, which she'd found adorable. Not that she'd say so. She sincerely doubted that a member of the mob would ever want to be referred to in such a manner, but he *was* adorable. He really was.

"I don't know. *Mamma* liked them. And I do enjoy creating them."

That day, he brought her a self-portrait and a charcoal sketch of his brother. While the resemblance had been dead on, she noticed that he'd depicted himself with many more shadows than he had his brother. Sandro had looked larger than life, almost heroic in his, while Tony's self-portrait was far smaller. He'd even drawn it on a sheet of paper that was half the size of Sandro's.

She considered asking him about this, but she didn't want him to think she was criticizing him. What he was able to do with nothing but charcoal and paper was so incredible. Also, she suspected that it took courage for him to bring his art pieces to her. She wanted to build him up rather than tear him down.

Admittedly another component of dating Tony that stirred her blood was the clandestine nature they'd chosen to go about it. Her parents knew she was dating someone, but she'd been purposely oblique about who he was. She knew, too, that Tony was hiding their relationship from his father, so everything about their dates had this extra edge to it. It was as if she was living out this secret life only she and Tony knew about. The exhilaration of this was something she'd never experienced before, and she'd been thriving on it, even as she felt guilty.

She knew she needed to tell her mom and dad soon.

It'd been a bit too easy to avoid coming clean with them because everything had been going magnificently. He'd already gone from feeling like a stranger to a friend, and even the term "friend" felt lacking. The way he called her *bellisima* made her melt inside. The words he said in that deep lilt of his were like the most decadent of desserts. She swore she could listen to him for hours on end and never, ever get tired of hearing him. He made her feel smart, too. And funny. And attractive.

No man had done that for her before. Back in New Orleans, she'd dated a handful of times, but the boys had never asked her out again. Not that those dates had been anything to write home about. What she remembered of them—and sometimes they'd been so boring she didn't remember much—were awkward and stilted. She'd agreed to those dates because the boys had asked her, but she hadn't felt particularly drawn to any of them. She'd just wanted to go out and have some fun. Maybe eat, go mini-golfing, or watch a movie.

Yet with Tony, she'd told him her hopes. She'd told him her dreams. It'd felt positively necessary to do so.

"I want to be a fully certified public accountant partly because I love numbers, but partly because it'll let me help people do their very best on their taxes. I want to make a positive difference in this world. I want what I do to matter, you know," she gushed out to him one afternoon in June.

He'd stared into her eyes as if analyzing her. He had such a gorgeous masculine face with his strong jaw and chin.

And those eyes. She didn't think she'd met anyone with the exact same hue of light golden brown as him. It made her want to write sonnets, and English had always been her worst subject.

They'd been outside looking through the moon roof of his Audi, studying the stars. It'd been one of those sultry Texas evenings, so he'd kept the windows up and the air conditioner on. He'd held her hand, tracing the shape of it like a child might outline their own palm with a pencil.

"What else?" he asked, softly.

"I want to travel the world in a hot air balloon, swim in the Salt Sea, stand on the edge of a volcano, and climb a glacier."

"Whoa. That's quite the ambitious list, *bellisima*."

"Yes. I figure if I'm going to dream, why not dream as big as possible? What about you?"

"Well, if I could, I'd have my *mamma* back again," he said, sounding wistful, and Kylie's heart broke for him. She'd wanted to go see the woman's grave with Tony, but since it was located on a site within the perimeter of the Menotti estate, such a visit wasn't likely to ever be possible. "But since I can't, I'd settle for my father to not discount me."

"Discount you? How does he discount you?"

Tony shook his head, looking like maybe he wished he hadn't said anything. "It's nothing."

"No, it's not. You can tell me. I tell you pretty much everything."

He kissed the back of her hand like he had the day they'd met. "He doesn't think much of me, my father. He's been grooming Sandro all his life, even from the time he was young, but he didn't bother with me. I realize that my brother is his heir and I'm not, but it's more than that. I've never felt like the patriarch considers me anything but extraneous. I'm just the extra son. The spare. I'm the kid who'd rather play violin and get my hands dirty with charcoal than get them dirty with the ins and outs of the business. Maybe if I'd shown an interest early on it'd be different, but it's not. That's the crux of it."

Kylie had mixed feelings about this. She knew that the Menotti family was in organized crime up to their eyeballs. They'd committed who knew how many illegal acts, so Tony wanting to be more involved with it gave her pause. But on the other side of the coin was knowing Tony as a person. The only reason he seemed interested at all was to get closer to his last surviving parent. She couldn't imagine losing either of her parents, but if she did, she could picture herself trying to get closer to the other. It made sense, even if she wanted to tell him not to.

Shelley had sent her some links to information about Viktor Menotti, and none of it had been encouraging. Though the man had never been convicted, he'd been arrested five times for crimes ranging from theft and embezzlement all the way up to arson and assault and battery. He'd managed to fight these charges well enough to be set free every single time, but Kylie couldn't help but think that the man had such a reputation for a reason.

"What about your art and music? Do you have any dreams concerning them?" she asked next.

"Sure. I used to, anyway. *Mamma* always encouraged me to pursue them and so did Sandro."

"You're closer to him than to your father, aren't you?"

"Oh, yes. Sandro perpetually made time for me growing up, even though there's a five-year gap in our ages. He's always been there for me, always been this buffer between me and *Papà*. He understands how I feel, even if he doesn't agree."

"He doesn't want you more involved?" Kylie pushed. If that were true, maybe she could turn Tony's brother into more of an ally. She'd come to care deeply about Tony— okay, well, actually she was totally head over heals for him, though she couldn't tell him—and she didn't want him to end up in either a jail cell or dead. She shuddered at both outcomes.

"No, which is ironic. It'll enable me to get closer to him, too, not just Father."

"Here's what I'm going to do," Kylie had said. "Tomorrow morning, I'm going to go up to the Law School fountain, toss a coin in, and wish for you to be what your mother wanted most. I think she'd want you to be safe because I know I do. How about that?"

His lips had curled up, but the cast to them was sad. "Fair enough. And I'll go up to the fountain at our estate and wish for all of your dreams to come true, no matter how ambitious."

She pecked him on the cheek again. "Fair enough."

"Honey," her mom called through her bedroom door, dragging Kylie back to the present. "Are you awake?"

"Yep. Come on in."

Bettina Cormier waltzed right in, a cheerful look on her face. "I just wanted to wish you a happy birthday. Are you sure you want to work today? We can make it without you if you want off."

"No, I don't mind." In truth, she'd volunteered to work today to keep herself busy. It was a Thursday, and Tony had said he wouldn't be available to celebrate with her. He'd apologized and told her he'd spend all day with her Saturday. She'd readily agreed, trying hard not to display the disappointment bubbling up within her. Times like these were when the whole secrecy thing got old.

"Come on downstairs, then, before we go. I've made your favorite."

"Pumpkin pie? I didn't even notice you baking it."

"Got up at five," she said proudly. "Your mom can still surprise you when she sets her mind to it."

"Ah, thank you so much." Kylie embraced her, feeling all warm and fuzzy inside. She threw on some clothes and headed downstairs. Her dad greeted her and handed her some coffee just the way she liked it. "Y'all are spoiling me."

"You deserve it, honey," her mom said, and her dad agreed, though he kept giving her long looks. What was that all about? "We're taking you out to dinner once we close. Know of anywhere specific you'd like to go?"

The image of the big sign for the Stuffed Potato popped into her head, but that was not where she said. "Anywhere is fine by me."

The three of them had just opened up Cormier's Cleaning and Alternations when one of their regular customers stuck his head into their door. "Have you noticed what's outside?"

Thinking nothing of it, Kylie asked about it without really caring. "No, what?"

"See for yourself," the guy said, pushing the door open for her. Since she had only a particular slice of the parking lot outside available for view, part of which was dominated by those dogwood trees, she left the area behind the counter to placate him.

Then, as soon as she stepped through the door, she gasped.

CHAPTER TWELVE

"HOLD IT RIGHT THERE, ZEB," TONY HALF SHOUTED, SO THE man could hear him over the noise. "Hopefully, I'll be right back."

As Tony raced away from the mammoth shadow the thing threw across the parking lot, he spotted the woman he'd created this whole spectacle for. She stood there outside her parents' business façade, her hands over her mouth as if stunned.

"Hi, *bellisima*," he greeted her, kissing her on the cheek. "Happy birthday."

She pointed at her surprise, her aqua blues round as saucers. "That's a… I… you…"

"Good to know you haven't been rendered incoherent," he quipped, chuckling.

"*Tony*." She put her hands on her hips as if attempting to be stern. He just thought it made her look cute. "That is a hot air balloon."

"Yes, it is. You get a gold star. Are you ready to go?"

"Go? Go where? I have to work."

"No, you don't," came her mother's voice from behind her, her hand raised over her eyes to block the sun. "That's pretty cool, there, Tony."

Kylie did an about-face, narrowing her eyes. "Since when are the two of you on a first-name basis?"

"Since he came to us yesterday and swore to take good care of you," her dad answered, his expression hard to read as he crossed his arms over his chest.

"He…" she glanced from her dad to Tony in utter confusion. "You… *what*?"

"I came to them while you were grocery shopping and explained the situation," Tony confessed, shoving down his nerves. This was the moment of truth.

"And you guys were okay with it? With Tony and I dating?" Kylie asked, doubt in her voice.

"It took some persuading," Tony said, unwilling to tell her just how persuasive he'd had to be. "But in the end, they both declared that they were okay with it."

"You did?" Kylie spun her head back around to face her parents. If she kept doing that, Tony worried that she might become dizzy.

"We were angry at first," Bettina eyed her husband. "Extremely angry, even. But then Tony told us how well you two had been getting along, and that he'd die before he ever endangered you."

"It was when he said he'd willingly die for you that I decided to give in," her dad said. He'd been a hard sale. "But if he ever steps a toe out of line, you let us know."

Kylie's mouth literally gaped open.

"I also told them one other thing." Tony stood directly in front of her and took her hands. "I told them that I love you."

"You do?" she whispered, staring up into his eyes.

"Very much," he whispered back. "I wanted to make your birthday memorable. You want to take a ride with me?"

"You sure it's okay for me to leave you shorthanded?" she asked her parents again, proving once more how dedicated of a daughter she was. Tony marveled at her.

"Yes," her mother repeated.

"Go," her father told her, his stiff posture relaxing by a few degrees. Tony knew the man would have his eyes on him for a long time probably, but he didn't mind.

Tony tugged at her hand. "Ready, birthday girl?"

"I…" she peered up and up and up at the enormous balloon. It was bright and colorful with literally every color in the rainbow represented in blocks that twisted on the diagonal. The balloon was nearly as brilliant as Kylie was. That was why he'd chosen it. "I guess so."

"Let's get aboard, then."

Finally, she quit looking like a deer in the headlights and started to look excited. "Okay."

Riding in a hot air balloon had not quite been what Tony had been anticipating. One, it was hot, like roasting-inside-a-deep-frier hot. Two, the basket they rode in was tighter than he'd been expecting. And three, as they ascended, Kylie began to cling to him, and by cling to him, he meant *climb* on him like a spider monkey.

"We're still going up," she said, over and over. "We're still going up."

"Are you okay? You seem noticeably scared right now," he deadpanned, as she literally hid her face in his armpit.

"I'm okay," she squeaked out, her arms around his neck as she attempted to jump on him piggyback style. "It's wonderful. It really is."

"*Bellisima…*" he paused as she almost choked him. "If you're afraid of heights, just say so."

"I'm not. Or at least I didn't used to be. But then again, I've never been in a hot air balloon before."

Tony signaled for Zeb, the operator, to level off. They were far enough above the city, anyway. "All right, we're not going any higher. Is that better?"

The ascent hadn't been anything but smooth, but for whatever reason, it had frightened her. Considerably. He continued to watch Kylie as she slowly disentangled from him, still staying in contact by holding his hand as she glimpsed over the side. "It's so beautiful," she yelped, trembling. "This is great."

It was a wonder why Tony didn't believe her.

"Kylie," he spoke, and she immediately pivoted to look at him, since he never referred to her by her real name. "We can go back down. You don't have to put some brave face on this."

"Wait, I just remembered something."

As he watched, she released him, widened her stance, pinched the skin between the forefinger and thumb of her left hand with her right index finger and thumb, and closed her eyes, breathing deeply. She stayed like that for several long seconds, but when she opened her eyes again, they seemed far more serene.

"You look less panicked now."

"It's an old trick I learned from my grandmother. It induces calm and relieves stress."

He pooched out his bottom lip. "Seems that it does. You truly feel better?"

"I do, I swear." It was her sweet giggle that made him believe her. "This is the most fantastic present I've ever gotten, Tony. Thank you."

Relieved to see her out of distress, he smiled. "You're more than welcome, *bellisima*."

"Oh, and that thing you told my parents?"

What thing? The truth about why they'd been hiding from them for so long?

"You know, the loving me thing?"

Ah, that thing. "Yes."

Then, she grabbed him by the lapels of his suit jacket. "I wanted to inform you about a new development of my own."

He wrapped his arms around her, gazing into those big, aqua blue eyes. "What's that?"

"I love you, too."

She stood up on her tippy-toes and pressed her lips to his. He tasted something sweet, like brown sugar, and relished it. It shouldn't be any huge mystery why she tasted sweet. It was simply who she was. When their kiss broke, it was because they were both grinning at one another. He felt as if the balloon were rising all over again, floating above the Earth and any problems that may be down there.

"Happy birthday, *bellisima*."

"How do you say happy birthday in Italian?"

"*Buon Compleanno*."

"*Buon Compleanno* to me, then." Kylie said the "buon" part like baaahn instead of boon, but he'd overlook it. He'd never felt so uplifted by another person before. That was how he knew he'd fallen for her, totally and completely.

Together, they peered over the side of the basket, taking in all the majesty of the city and even portions of the farm-lands extending beyond. It made for a pretty picture as they floated there suspended, and since the woman he loved had calmed down, he felt loath to return to the reality of his life.

As if his feelings had been a portent of something bad happening, within minutes of leaving the balloon and watching it drift back toward where he'd rented it from, his cell phone rang. He glanced at the display to see *Papà* on the screen. His father almost never contacted him. In fact, he could count on one hand the number of times he had. And every single one of those times had been because either he'd been displeased with him or he'd had horrible news to impart.

He answered, "*Papà*?"

"I need you home, Antonio."

Normally, he would comply without question, but he'd had plans with Kylie for the day. "Is something wrong?"

"I'd say so," his father said gruffly, a growl in his tone. "Your brother's been shot."

CHAPTER THIRTEEN

AT FIRST, ALL TONY COULD HEAR WAS RINGING IN HIS EARS. Sandro had been shot? The words simply would not compute. They refused to.

"Is he alive?" his voice left him in a high-pitched rasp.

"Yes, but I want you home. Now."

Knowing this would be all he could get out of the patriarch on the phone, he answered with an obedient, "Yes, sir."

Then, he turned around and found Kylie. The last thing he wanted to do was leave her high and dry—especially after that kiss and on her birthday of all days—but he had little choice in the matter. "I'm so sorry, but I have to go."

"What happened?"

"My brother has been shot. He's alive but I don't know any additional details."

Her expression became instantly serious and determined. "Go to him. Don't worry about me. Just call later with any updates you have, okay?"

He nodded his head, his bones aching with icy dread, as he twisted away from her. "All right."

"Tony," she called him back. He stopped and faced her again. "I love you."

"Love you, too." Then, he sprinted to his Audi, squealing his tires as he gunned it back across town.

When he arrived home, he found their head of security, a man named Benito, at the front door. "Your brother is in his bedroom, Master Antonio." Patting his arm in thanks, Tony ran up to the second floor to his brother's living space.

In the hallway outside his rooms, his father materialized, looking ready to leave.

"*Papà*, how is he?"

"He will live. The bullet struck him in the arm." The patriarch appeared to be in a hurry.

Tony let out a gust of relief. "Are you going somewhere?" he asked without thinking. The movements of the head of their *famiglia* were not to be discussed or questioned.

"I have matters to attend to elsewhere," Viktor replied coldly, and a couple of beats later, he was gone.

Without giving his father much more thought, Tony burst into Sandro's quarters. He found him on his bed as Pietro sat on one side and Dante on the other. His cousins looked… sheepish. His brother had a roll of gauze wrapped around the biceps and triceps of his left arm, though some blood had leaked through. Motioning for Dante to hand him another roll, Pietro doubled the amount of bandages as if hoping to stop the bleeding.

"Sandro," Tony spoke his name to let him know he was there since his brother's eyes had been closed. Pietro got up from his seat to make room for him, his complexion paler than usual. "What happened?"

"Boccias," was all Sandro said. He seemed a little out of it, and his cheeks seemed abnormally flushed.

"The Boccias did this to you? I'll *murder* them."

"You'll do no such thing," his brother said sternly, sounding clearer-headed. "You're not ready to go out and about with guns blazing."

"Yes, I am. I've been training with these two." Tony indicated his two cousins. "I can take the Boccias. This can't stand."

"It can," Sandro argued. "I'll be all right. We got the bullet out even though it was in more than one piece. It hurts like you know what, but I'll survive."

Tony yanked his hands through his hair. "I can't believe they did this. Where did it happen?"

"Downtown. We were doing some errands," Pietro chimed in. He sounded as shaken as Tony felt.

"Can I get you anything? Some water? Some food?" Tony asked him, though he felt close to passing out with worry.

Sandro is okay, he told himself, chanting it like a mantra. *Sandro is okay*.

"No, *fratello*. I just need to rest. Tomorrow I'll be as good as new."

But the next day, Sandro *wasn't* as good as new. Tony shooed out his cousins and stayed up to watch his brother as he slept, then ultimately at around two in the morning, left to go to his own rooms and rest. He regretted this the instant he ambled back in after only about five hours of sleep, because he found his brother in his bed sweating and writhing on his mattress. Pietro and Dante stood there doing nothing, so Tony tore into them.

"Why are you just standing there? Can't you see he's sick?" Even the room smelled of illness, of something gone bad. Tony reached out and laid his palm on his brother's forehead, immediately yanking it back. "He's burning up. Dangerously so."

Without hesitation, Tony grabbed at his phone and dialed 911.

Once ensconced in the Intensive Care Unit of LifeCare Hospital, they started an IV and began to run tests. Since space was so limited, only one family member at a time was allowed in, which meant Tony stayed in there alone. He'd told his father what was happening, but other than grunting at him, he hadn't reacted. Fed up with him, Tony had disconnected and gone back to focusing on Sandro.

His brother squirmed in the twin-sized bed, tearing at his hospital gown and generally appearing miserable. His skin looked as scarlet as if he'd been sunburned despite his olive complexion, and his injured arm had terrifying red lines streaking out from the top and bottom of his bandages like lightning strikes. He was mumbling about something Tony couldn't understand, so he knelt closer, trying to hear him.

"What did you say, *fratello*? I didn't catch that. Please, say it again."

"Boccias… Boccias…."

"What about the Boccias?"

"Boccias," he echoed, clearly so feverish as to be delirious.

Tony sat in a terribly uncomfortable plastic hospital chair and put his head in his hands. He didn't notice the large cream tiles beneath his feet or the green on the walls that reminded him rather disgustingly of pea soup. Losing his older brother and mentor was something he could not do. Not now. Not so soon after losing their mother. He'd experienced too much grief and loss to be capable of dealing with more of it.

"Boccias…" Sandro muttered. "Boccias… reason for *Mamma's* car wreck…"

"What?" Tony exclaimed.

"Always suspected… too convenient… not an accident… foul play…"

"What do you mean, Sandro? Talk to me." But his brother only stared at him with overbright eyes and a sweat-ravaged countenance.

"Antonio…"

"Yes?"

"*Antonio…*" He reached out with his good arm and seized Tony's hand.

"Yeah, *fratello*, I'm right here."

"I love you."

Although they'd been close, his brother had never actually said those words to him before now.

"I… I love you, too, Sandro."

"Don't do this. Please."

"Don't do what?"

"Be involved in Menotti crime business. Swear to me you won't."

But before Tony could say anything else, his brother stopped floundering on his mattress and went still. Tony pressed his palm to his forehead, then pushed his damp raven locks back out of his face. Sandro didn't speak again, though. He'd slipped into unconsciousness.

In the next moment, a doctor wearing a white coat and blue scrubs came up to the foot of Sandro's bed carrying a chart. "Mr. Menotti?"

"Yes, I'm Antonio Menotti, Alessandro's brother," Tony explained, even though his brain was still reeling from what he'd just heard.

"I'm Dr. Neil Cohen. Your brother is showing signs of sepsis and X-rays are showing some sort of foreign object in his wound. We have to take him to surgery."

"Now?"

"Yes, sir."

As Tony watched helplessly, Dr. Cohen and a couple of orderlies took Sandro's bed and wheeled it straight out of the room and down a corridor. They vanished through some double swinging doors at the end of the artificially lit hall. Tony stared after them, wondering if he'd ever see his beloved big brother alive again.

Tony had been sitting in the waiting room next to his two cousins for he had no idea how long. For once, the two men were quiet, barely speaking except to check on him. But Tony didn't respond. Even when his father at last showed his face in the waiting room, sitting down across from his youngest son, Tony didn't look up. His phone vibrating in his pocket hardly registered, either. He was too lost in the horrifying thought that Sandro might lose this battle.

Also, he couldn't stop analyzing what his brother had said. It sounded as if he'd known something about their mother's car accident that he hadn't divulged until now. The words that stuck with Tony the most were "Boccias" and "foul play."

At the time, investigators had not been able to determine any foul play that Tony had known of, and since those members of law enforcement were on the Menotti payroll, he'd felt like they were telling the truth. But what if there had been more to it than that? What if Sandro somehow had some secret inside knowledge that he'd been keeping under wraps? It'd be just like his brother to conceal something from Tony to protect him.

If Sandro had just let something vital slip, and the Boccias were responsible for his *mamma's* death…

Tony clenched his fists, feeling a combustible fury he'd never before known. If those goons had murdered his mother, he would kill them, no ifs, ands, or buts. He would avenge her or die trying.

"Antonio, look," Pietro nudged him with his elbow, and Tony glanced up to catch sight of Sandro's physician coming through the doors with a grim expression on his face. Fear streaked through his system matched only by his dread. Not Sandro, too…

On legs he couldn't feel, Tony somehow managed to rise to his feet. Without preamble, Dr. Cohen strode over to him, his posture showing heavy fatigue.

"We were able to remove the bullet fragments," he didn't mince words by calling the foreign object anything but what it was. "But once we were inside, there were complications. He tried to bleed out on us twice, and we were barely able to contain it. The bullet apparently shattered on impact because it hit his humerus, fracturing the bone where an infection settled in. We've had him on antibiotics ever since he arrived, but it wasn't enough. Unfortunately, we had to amputate."

"You amputated his arm?" Tony asked, not recognizing his own voice. He didn't sound anything like himself.

"I'm afraid we had no other option, Mr. Menotti. It was remove the arm or let him die."

"Is he going to be all right?"

"Frankly, it's still too early to tell. We did everything we could in the operating room. We're hoping now that with the infection site being taken out of the equation, his body will be able to heal. We'll continue to monitor him closely."

"Can I see him?"

"He's in the process of being transferred to recovery now, but he'll probably stay asleep for the next several hours. I'd rather him rest for now. I'll have a nurse come out and escort you to him once he's awake."

The doctor wandered off, and Tony sat with his head in his hands again. Sometime later he felt his phone buzzing against his leg again. Feeling antsy, he pulled his cell out of his pocket and checked the screen. It was Kylie. Since he needed to hear the sound of her voice, he did a brief scan to make certain his father wasn't around to overhear him, then picked up.

"*Bellisima.*"

"Tony, thank goodness. Are you okay? Is Sandro? What happened? I've been freaking out. I'm so glad you answered," she blurted out so fast it all ran together.

"Slow down a little," he told her and might've smiled had he not been so concerned about everything himself. "I'm fine, but Sandro..." He tried to spit it out twice, but there was an inconvenient lump in his throat. "They had to amputate his arm," he eventually told her in a voice full of gravel.

"Oh, no. I'm so, so sorry."

"He's not out of the woods yet, either. They don't know if taking out the source of the infection will be enough to rid his body of it or not." He paused, then voiced the thought that had emerged just that moment in his head. "I wish you were here."

"I'll come if you want, even though it is three in the morning."

"It's three in the morning?" he asked, shocked by this. Through the waiting room windows he'd seen that it'd become dark outside, but he hadn't comprehended the passage of time despite having his phone in his pocket. For the first time in he didn't know how long, Tony peeked down at his watch. Since he'd last seen his brother, it'd been over fifteen hours.

"Yes. I only called at this hour because I can't sleep. I've been so concerned about you."

"Thank you, *bellisima*. It means a lot to know you're thinking of me."

"I love you, Tony. Of course I've been thinking of you. I've done nothing but."

She said this with such conviction that he felt a little better. Just then, Pietro trudged by, looking bedraggled. The last time he'd seen his two cousins, they'd been sleeping in the waiting room. He muted his phone.

"Pietro, what do you know about *Mamma's* car accident?"

"What do you mean?" His cousin stiffened his spine, looking suddenly green around the gills. To Tony, this read like a dead giveaway, especially when Pietro reached into his pocket to extract one of his lollipops and straight up dropped the thing on the tiled floor.

"I mean that she was murdered because that so-called accident of hers was anything but. And apparently, you've known this all along."

Pietro bent to pick up his Dum Dum, shaking his head in denial, but Tony stormed off anyway. He was so enraged at his cousin. At his entire *famiglia*. Had everyone known except for him? Sandro and Pietro, for sure, which meant Dante likely did, too. Did his father know? Why hadn't he retaliated against the rivals who'd stolen his wife away from him? The mother of his children? A million kinds of turmoil and stress reigned in his mind. He felt like he must take some sort of action, but he didn't know what it should be.

Only then did he see his phone in his hand and remembered that he'd muted Kylie. Taking a deep breath so he wouldn't sound as insane as he felt, he touched the button to unmute her.

"Are you there? Tony?"

"I apologize. I'm here."

"Did something happen with Sandro?"

"No. He's still the same. They're keeping him in the ICU and allowing him no visitors for now."

"Which hospital did you take him to? I want to be there for you."

The idea of having her there was too good to pass up. Viktor must've gone home at some point because he hadn't seen him around for hours. It wasn't exactly a tough decision to make after that. "LifeCare. On Record Crossing Road."

"I'm on my way."

CHAPTER FOURTEEN

"*Bellisima...*" Tony said, embracing Kylie tightly. A little too tightly, in all honesty, but she wasn't about to complain. All she'd done for the past twenty-four hours was drive herself up every wall in her house with anxiety over him, particularly when he didn't answer any of the ten—yes, *ten*—calls she made to him. She'd also left five voicemails that he hadn't responded to. Maybe that was why she'd felt almost faint with relief when he finally did answer her call.

When he released her, she continued to clasp on to his elbows as she regarded him at arm's length. She'd always thought of Tony Menotti as a handsome man, even when she'd wanted to hate him, and ironically that handsomeness made his pallor and general state of exhaustion even more prevalent. His complexion had this almost waxy look to it with dark half circles under his eyes, and his posture was slumped, as if he could barely keep upright.

Despite this, though, he was fidgety. He kept shifting his weight back and forth from one foot to the other and moving in odd little ways that were unusual for him. He rubbed his eyebrow, scratched the back of his neck, and speared his hand through his hair as she stood there watching. He was understandably worried about his brother, but this struck Kylie as something beyond worried. He seemed all keyed up. Frazzled and upset.

"Tony, are you okay? Is Sandro going to be all right?" she asked, observing him closely.

He pressed his lips together, his nostrils flaring and his forehead marred with a long, vertical line. Was he angry, too?

"I hope so. He… he's out of surgery, but I haven't been able to see him yet."

"I'm sure they'll let you back there as soon as they can," she told him. He nodded but trying to reassure him didn't seem to have any impact. "Come over here and sit with me."

She led him over to a nearby seating area with chairs that had no armrests so they could stay in proximity with one another. To give herself more height, she positioned herself with one leg crossed beneath her, wrapping an arm around him and tugging his head down so it rested on her shoulder. He let her maneuver him around, not fighting or resisting her in any way. She kissed his temple, and he looped his arms around her waist as if desperate for the physical contact.

He quit fiddling around and relaxed, and she sighed. Since it was the middle of the night, the hospital was mostly silent. She and Tony were the only people in the waiting area, and with the exception of a few medical staff and a single custodian mopping a section of floor, no one else even entered their vicinity.

Kylie breathed in the lightly spicy scent of his hair and the faint, more distant tang of the disinfectant the janitor was using and let herself relax as well. It felt so natural to hold him like this, to be there for him like this. These were horrible circumstances, no doubt, but she treasured this time to support the man she loved when he so clearly needed her.

He'd been so quiet for so long that she thought he'd drifted off to sleep. But when he spoke, he sounded anything but sleepy. "Sandro told me a secret before they took him to surgery."

"Yeah?"

"Yes. He told me my mother's car accident might've been caused by the Boccias." Kylie stiffened. That was a pretty huge bomb his brother had dropped on him. "I haven't been able to think about anything else since."

Wow. Kylie remained speechless for a minute. She simply didn't know what to say. Finally, she thought of something, though it wasn't exactly profound. "That sounds like disturbing news."

"It is. I don't know what to do with it, with the knowledge that possibly everyone knew but me."

"Do you know that for sure?"

"No. Sandro was… not well at the time. But that's all the more reason why I think it's true. Because he's the older brother, he's had this habit of protecting me. I think he's kept this information a secret for that purpose. I doubt he would've told me otherwise. I don't think he wanted me to know."

"Isn't that honorable, though?" she suggested. "I mean, it's misguided, too, because you're a grown man who has every right to know, but he was trying to watch out for you."

"Perhaps."

They didn't speak for a while after that, and Kylie found her eyelids growing heavier and heavier. She hadn't slept at all, and now, it was all catching up to her. Tony was a warm, comforting weight against her side, and she closed her eyes to rest them.

Somehow, she must've fallen into a doze. She felt peaceful and content until a deep voice she'd never heard before spoke right above her.

"What is the meaning of this?"

The question hadn't been a shout or any louder than regular speaking volume, but it was enough to wake both her and Tony. They each jolted upwards in their seat as if they'd been tasered. Flustered, she made to move away from Tony, but her man seized her arm, not letting her go.

Kylie peeked up to the speaker of that deep voice to see a man with black hair with silver at the temples and equally dark eyes glaring down at her. He had this subtly frightening demeanor about him, and behind him stood the two men from the Menotti family she'd met that day back in April.

"*Papà*, this is my girlfriend, Kylie Cormier. *Bellisima*, this is my father, Viktor, the patriarch of the Menotti family."

"Girlfriend, you say," Viktor said, full on sneering at her. "Yet this is the first I've heard of..." he trailed off. "Wait, why does that name sound familiar? Cormier?" He turned to point his laser-like gaze at one of the men behind him.

Tony gripped her arm more firmly, but other than that, he gave no outward sign of what he might be feeling. One of the men—she knew his name must be either Dante or Pietro—answered, "Her parents run Cormier's Cleaning and Alterations, one of the businesses we protect, Uncle."

Viktor's expression betrayed no shock or disapproval, but when he focused all his attention on his son, his change of attitude made Kylie want to duck and run for cover. "Send her away."

"What? *Papà,* I..."

"A stranger to our *famiglia* should not be here. This is a private affair, as you well know. It is inappropriate to have outsiders involved, for them to know things they shouldn't."

Without giving Tony a chance for any rebuttal, Viktor pivoted on his heel and whisked away, his suit-clad form aimed to vanish down a side corridor. Before he disappeared from view completely, Tony released Kylie and stood, his fists clenched and his body visibly quaking. Not with fear, though, she could tell. The rigid lines of his stance told her this was pure outrage.

"Strangers aren't the only ones you've been keeping in the dark, are they, *Papà*?" Viktor Menotti stopped, still facing forward, away from his son. "You and everyone else have been hiding what really happened to *Mamma* from me. I'm her son, and I deserved to know. Moreover, you, as her husband and my father, should've been the one to enlighten me."

Excruciatingly slowly, Viktor pivoted back around, his face a storm cloud on the cusp of breaking. He lumbered over to Tony with his head held high, his steps purposeful and deliberate, halting within a couple of feet of him. "I have no notion of what it is you're saying, but I will not stand for your speaking to me like this. You shall not question me about the decisions I make for this *famiglia*, especially not in public. You should know your place by now, Antonio."

"My place is right here at the hospital where my brother nearly died. Where my mother *did* die. And apparently, all due to the same people you refuse to go after. Why won't you make a move against them, seek vengeance for what they've done? Not to strike back at them makes us look weak."

If Kylie had thought Viktor looked menacing before, it had nothing on how he looked now. His features twisted, his skin warping into an even nastier version of its already intimidating expression. If she hadn't been so terrified for Tony, she would've scampered out of there in a heartbeat. Viktor Menotti had "dangerous and powerful felon" written all over him. Tony's two cousins had situated themselves off to the side between father and son, watching the tense proceedings like a tennis match.

"How dare you attempt to dictate to me. Who do you think you are, anyway?"

"I'm the one who's going to do what you should've done already. I'm going to go avenge my mother and brother."

With that, Tony marched right past his father and away from the scene. Viktor, resembling a grenade with its pin pulled, barreled off in the opposite direction, Pietro and Dante following him at a distance. Shakily, Kylie got to her feet. She couldn't let Tony go off and get himself killed no matter what the Boccias had done or how livid he felt. Jogging as fast as she dared through the hospital's hallways, she bolted after him.

CHAPTER FIFTEEN

TONY HAD NEVER FELT SO INFURIATED IN ALL HIS LIFE, AND although he knew he might later regret spewing like an exploding volcano all over his father, at that precise second, he didn't care. His ire still sped through his veins like poison, and what he felt most compelled to do was mow down every last member of the Boccia Crime Syndicate until they ceased to exist anymore. That single heinous thought had just zoomed through his brain when he heard Kylie's voice.

"Tony!" she yelled, waving at him from the hospital's main entrance. "Tony, wait!" He was already halfway across the parking lot with his Audi in sight, but he paused, delaying his progress for her. Her light brown hair was mussed even though she'd put it up in a ponytail, and her pink sweatpants and T-shirt were wrinkled. He might have thought her adorable had the situation not been so dire. As soon as she reached him, she grabbed at his arm, out of breath. "What are you doing?"

"What I must. I can't stand by and do nothing. I'm not going to be able to live with myself until I take care of this."

"But they might kill you."

"Don't you think I know that?" he growled out, his eyes flying back to his vehicle. Why didn't she understand how important this was to him? This felt like a cross for him to bear, one—for whatever reason—no one else had seemed obliged to carry. And he'd see this to its end, even if it cost him everything. He'd prove to his father, his cousins, and himself that he was capable and determined enough to be a real Menotti. No one would doubt him ever again. "I can't let this go. I *won't*."

Kylie dropped his arm, and he glanced down at her. Tears had brimmed in her beautiful blue eyes, and for the first time, he felt a tendril of uncertainty crawl up his spine.

"Tony, I love you, and I know you've had a really rough day or two. But I'm not okay with this, and I'm not just going to go mind the counter at work and pretend that I am. We need to discuss this, to talk it out."

"There's nothing to discuss," he argued.

"I think there is."

"You're wrong."

"You're upset and irrational," she volleyed back.

Why was she making this so much more difficult? He had to do this. He didn't have a choice in the matter.

"I'm not going to stand out here and fight with you about this, Kylie."

At his use of her real name, she planted her hands on her hips. "Antonio Menotti, you listen to me right now. This little quest of yours will do nothing to bring your mother back or heal your brother. So either you let this vendetta of yours go, or you let *me* go."

He stared at her, immobilized with indecision. He'd never imagined her saddling him with this ridiculous ultimatum, but that was precisely what she'd done. Because this had hit him from so far out of left field, he hadn't suspected it was coming. But the more he accepted the reality of it, the more it felt like treachery, like her attempting to use his own emotions to manipulate him.

And he couldn't have a woman by his side who'd manipulate him like this at such a crucial juncture.

Squaring his shoulders, he firmed his resolve. She must've been able to read his decision in his face because two fat tears leaked from the corners of her eyes, streaming down her cheeks. But he wouldn't be moved by them. He couldn't be.

Instead, he turned and closed the distance to his sportscar. Jumping inside, he started the engine, which came alive in a mechanical roar, and clamored off out of the hospital's parking lot, purposely avoiding looking in his rearview. Navigating to the Menotti estate, he bit out a demand for Bruno to let him through the gate, then careened up the driveway. Braking so hard that his tires let out a noisy screech, he sprang out of the Audi without even bothering to shut his driver's side door.

Busting into his home, he rushed straight over to the closet-like room buried deep within the bowels of the first floor, the room everyone referred to as the armory. Plugging in a code no one probably even realized he knew, he belted on a double holster, grabbed two separate hand pistols, and loaded each of them with as many bullets as they could carry.

He threw some extra magazines that would clip on his guns into the inner pockets of his suit jacket, so he wouldn't run out before getting the job done. Then, just to be safe, he snagged an automatic rifle and several magazines for it, too. Satisfied, he slammed the door shut and rearmed the security mechanism, then headed back out.

His phone rang and he glanced at the screen, but it was only Pietro. Nothing he couldn't avoid. As he drove across town toward the Boccia mansion, he received three additional calls from Pietro and two from Dante. He didn't care. Whatever they had to say could wait. Nothing mattered as much as going through with this mission. Once finished, he'd be able to say with impunity that no one cared more about his *famiglia* than he did, which was true. Nothing had ever felt truer.

Tony had pulled up beside what looked to be a fortress. The walls around the Boccia estate were even higher and thicker in appearance than the ones guarding the Menotti residence, so he knew he'd have to have a plan. He drove around the perimeter slowly, looking for a way in. Perhaps if he snuck in the back...

His phone rang again, and he gusted out a frustrated breath. Why wouldn't his aggravating cousins just leave him alone? But then he caught sight of the name on his cell and paused. It wasn't Pietro or Dante calling this time. It was Sandro.

Instantly, he connected the call.

"*Fratello*?"

"Ah, Antonio, it's good to hear your voice."

"It's even better to hear yours. Are you all right?" He didn't ask about his arm. He couldn't seem to get those particular words out of his mouth.

"Well," he chuckled mirthlessly. "I may have a new name."

"A new name?" Tony asked in puzzlement. He'd thought that Sandro sounded lucid and alert, but maybe he'd been mistaken. Had he become feverish again?

"The one-armed wonder."

A joke. His brother was definitely doing better, all things considered.

"Oh. Are you… does it…" Tony had to pause to figure out what it was he wanted to ask. "Is the infection gone?"

"Yes. I'm all clear on that. I've lost my arm but gained my life. I suppose that's a relatively fair trade when I think about it."

"Yes," he agreed at a whisper.

His brother was going to live. Tony hunched forward in the seat of his car, overwhelmed by the massive amount of relief that rolled over him then. He felt a suspicious burning at the back of his eyes and nose that he didn't want to contemplate. Deep down, he'd been horrifyingly afraid that the surgery wouldn't be enough, that Sandro wouldn't live through this, after all. Now that he had evidence that his assumption had been wrong, he felt less than sure about the goal he'd set for himself.

"Our dear cousins have informed me that you left the hospital in a hurry. Where are you going?"

If his cousins had told his brother that Tony left, Sandro knew where he was going. Where he'd already gone.

"I…" To his frustration, he suddenly felt more tentative about this than he wanted to. To circumvent this, he spoke hastily. "I need to avenge the wrongs done to our *famiglia*. I have to, so I'm going to have to let you go now."

Let him go. Just like he'd let Kylie go.

The thought made something acutely painful fill the space directly behind his ribcage, but he couldn't think about Kylie right now. He couldn't think about anything but the task at hand. The task that seemed far less appealing than it had five minutes ago.

"*Fratello*," his brother said softly. So softly Tony had to concentrate to hear him. "Why do you think that the Boccias are responsible for *Mamma*?"

Why? "Because that's what you told me."

"I don't recall this conversation. When did it occur?"

"When we were at the hospital. Before your surgery."

"Antonio, I hardly remember anything from yesterday, least of all a discussion about our mother's car accident."

"But—"

Sandro cut Tony off. "I wasn't in my right mind, so whatever I may have rambled about has no validity."

"You're telling me that the Boccias aren't responsible for sabotaging *Mamma* on her way home? That they're not responsible for you losing your arm?"

"What I'm telling you is that I'd rather not discuss this over the phone. You need to go home. Or come back to see me. They're transferring me to my own room within the hour."

Tony said nothing. How could he drop this after everything that had happened?

"Do you even know how many people work for the Boccias?" Sandro asked next. "How big their organization is? Should you go there by yourself, you shall be outnumbered at least four to one, though it's likely the odds will be even worse. It would be suicide, *fratello*, and I cannot live with that. Come back to us. Come back before you pass the point of no return. Whatever you might do to them, you will not survive it. And then, we will end up in a full-scale war. What would be the outcome of that, do you think? Do you believe I have a shot at defeating anybody while I'm still healing? Think of the position you would be putting us all in."

Tony could picture it all too easily. His family facing off with the Boccias. Sandro insisting on participating for retribution's sake. Even with his father and cousins lining up beside all their hired guns, there would be casualties on both sides, and a turf war would also be difficult to conceal from others. What if someone not on their payroll reported it? Busted their crime ring wide open? What if they were captured and put before an unbiased judge? All of them being in prison would be little better than all or most of them dying on the pavement somewhere.

And just like that, Tony's thirst for revenge evaporated. Suddenly, he didn't even know what he was doing there outside the walls of the Boccia estate. He couldn't win this, so what would his death prove? What if Sandro was right about the ramifications going off on his own like this might cause?

Nudging his accelerator, Tony drove carefully away from the Boccias' home.

"You're right," he admitted to his brother.

"As usual."

"You're also arrogant."

This time when Sandro chuckled it sounded sincere. "Admittedly. But that's just because I know everything."

Tony snorted, then grimaced. "I, uh… may have had a bit of a falling out with the patriarch."

"Yes, I've heard. I suggest avoiding him for a while."

"And with Kylie."

"You've made quite a mess of things, haven't you?"

"Thanks for your support," Tony said sardonically.

"You know you'll always have it," his brother said candidly. "When will I see you?"

"Soon," Tony promised, then disconnected.

Next to him on the seat lay the rifle and ammunition he'd brought, glinting dimly in the sunlight muted by his heavy window tint. Before his mother had died, he never would've considered doing something like this. Feeling unsettled and regretful, he found himself not driving to the hospital, though. Instead, he headed home, not going into the gigantic main house but to the back corner of the property. To the place where his mother's remains had been laid.

Once there, he knelt beside her gravestone. With pure reverence, his fingers traced the bold outline of the letters of his mother's name.

ELLIANA AVA MINICHIELLO-MENOTTI

BELOVED WIFE AND MOTHER

"Hi, *Mamma*," he mumbled as a sultry summer breeze blew over him. "I haven't come to see you since the funeral, and I'm sorry about that. I guess..." he paused, the burning behind his nose and eyes back. "I guess I couldn't. I've been twisting myself in knots over what happened to you, about not having you here anymore, and I've messed a lot of things up. Now, I don't know what to do."

"I wasn't ready to lose you. Maybe I never would've been, but having you gone so young..." His mother had only been forty-seven. "It feels wrong. Maybe I wanted to blame someone, to take it out on them. Having a target let me feel a little better about it, like if I could just kill whoever was responsible, it wouldn't hurt so much anymore. That probably sounds awful, but it's true. Even if I suppose I always knew it wouldn't actually work like that."

Wetness seeped in a path down either side of his nose, across his lips, and off his chin. He didn't pay it any mind, though his voice sounded clogged, as if mostly blocked. Still, he went on.

"The only bright spot in my life has been a woman named Kylie. We met in an awkward way, but she's been so beneficial to me. She's so kind, so beautiful. Father doesn't approve, but I think you would. I *know* you would." More wetness sluiced down his face, becoming thicker and blurring his vision, but he was determined to continue. "I'm in love with her. She's the one. But I've ruined everything." A sob interrupted him, followed by another. He paused to let them pass, speaking again once he was able.

"I don't know if there is an afterlife, a heaven. Though if there is, I know that's where you are. Sometimes, I could swear that I feel you near, like you're right beside me, even. Maybe I just want you to be. But if you are, if you can hear me and can give me any guidance here, I'd really appreciate it."

Another light gust blew over him, but this time it was cooler and from the polar opposite direction. It was a tiny thing, something he could dispute as real by putting it down to coincidence or happenstance, but he didn't. This time he *knew* his mother was there with him in spirit. He felt soothed. Comforted. As he knelt there, scrubbing his sorrow from his face, a solution came into his mind.

And he smiled in gratitude because now, he knew what to do.

CHAPTER SIXTEEN

KYLIE'S TRIP HOME FROM THE HOSPITAL HAD BEEN A BLUR. She'd been so taken aback by Tony's abrupt choice to go after the Boccias rather than doing something—anything—that would've been a safer alternative that she walked all the way back home like a victim of shellshock. As if watching herself from a distance, she assumed part of her dazed state came from not getting enough rest, so she'd fallen onto her mattress the second she reached her bedroom.

It didn't work, though. She'd lain there facedown, eyes closed, waiting patiently for oblivion to take her, but it never did. Instead, her mind spun like her mom's thick spools of thread on her sewing machine. Kylie had been crying in the parking lot of LifeCare, but as she'd ambled home, her tears had stopped.

Now, she felt blank. Not numb, because numbness would've felt better than this. Numbness to her was the absence of pain, the total cessation of it. But that wasn't how she felt. She felt as blank as an unused and disregarded sheet of notebook paper. She felt as if prior to meeting Tony she'd been this fully fledged person, but now, she wasn't. Somehow, it was as if everything pertinent about her had been erased like it'd never existed in the first place.

So despite her exhaustion flattening her like a steamroller, she remained inexcusably awake. It might've been exasperating if she'd had the ability to feel anything. She thought about her Uncle Kyle. Before the onset of his dementia, he'd led such an interesting life. He'd gone on safari in Africa, attempted—and failed—to climb Mount Everest, taken an Alaskan cruise to see a pod of humpbacks, and hiked the length of the Great Wall in China.

And what had she as Kyle's namesake done with her life so far? Precious little. It was actually absurd to her how little she had done. Granted, she was only twenty-one, and she had lots of time for future adventures. She could still do all the things her uncle had done. Or she could do totally different things. She could backpack through Europe. She could ski in the Swiss Alps. She could be a tourist in Tokyo. She could do all the things she'd mentioned before, including finishing her degree to become the CPA she'd always wanted to be.

Or she could stay attached to that front counter of Cormier's Cleaning and Alterations for the rest of her life.

For the first time ever, the thought of that sounded torturous. That building, beyond being her parents' livelihood, was the place where she'd initially crossed paths with Tony Menotti and the memory of him clung to it like Velcro. That was a problem now that he'd left her. Now that he'd gone off to do this ill-considered venture that would most likely result in his death. Because, as she sat at that counter, all her memories of that man would ultimately come back to haunt her.

He would always haunt her.

Almost idly, she contemplated what he was doing right that moment. Was he preparing for his absurd "assault?" Was he already on his way? Had everything already happened, whatever violence that he'd planned to make transpire? Had he been taken prisoner by them? Had he been injured? Or was he already dead?

She pictured it without meaning to. Tony, lying in a casket, all peaceful, no real damage to his body visible, but, as the man she loved, irretrievably gone. Not stolen from her, either. Not taken. He'd given his life to that other band of rival thugs, and for what? What had he hoped to accomplish? He'd thrown her love and his own life away laboring under the delusion that it would, what? Make his family whole again by reversing time?

His decision wasn't just bad, it had no valid point. It was useless. An unforgivable waste.

She should be mad at him. She should be thrashing about her bedroom destroying things left and right, and yet she wasn't. She was still lying there on her bed like a slug as the world revolved on without her. Or was it? How could the world keep rotating when the man that she loved, the man that she'd stood by and tried to support, had abandoned her for no other reason than to go off and get slaughtered?

Her chest burned, and she couldn't breathe right, so she sat up. Only then did she realize that she was making noise. Somehow the blankness had given way to weeping without her registering the fact. She grabbed at the box of tissues she kept by her bedside and attempted to stem the flow of her tears, but they just kept on coming. Her breathing had become ragged—no, it'd been ragged for a while—but she couldn't stop choking on all the horror and sorrow that came with losing a guy she never should've fallen for to begin with.

Her bedroom door opened, and she glanced up.

"Kylie, honey, I've been knocking and calling through your door. Didn't you hear me? What's wrong?"

Her mom. Her mom was there. And her dad was standing behind her, his face a mask of concern.

"T-Tony," Kylie stuttered out, her crying hindering her ability to speak properly.

"What did he do?" her dad asked, his tone antagonistic.

"H-he went off to fight the Boccias. All by himself. He's probably dead by now." That horrible revelation dislodged everything else, and she told her parents the truth about their relationship. How it'd been more than just a date. How it'd started based on a "deal." How he'd agreed to deduct a certain amount from their payments in order to keep having dates with her.

"I told you these thugs wouldn't just *forget* to come back and charge their ludicrous 'protection money.' I told you it was too good to be true," her father said to her mother. Obviously, this had been a point of contention between them Kylie hadn't known about.

But her mom merely waved her husband off and addressed her daughter. "So you're saying you negotiated with Tony Menotti to keep us from owing them? That you sacrificed yourself to save your father and me?"

"Well," Kylie gasped out, doing her best to regain her composure. "Yeah. I mean, I had to help you guys, or the business might've gone under. What else could I do?"

"Nothing," her father answered sternly. "You could've done nothing. It isn't your responsibility to step in and—for heaven's sake, Kylie—risk your life for a few bucks a month."

"It was more than a few bucks," she objected.

"I don't care if they wanted to charge us a *million* a month. It's not your place to put a target on your back. That's the last thing we would ever want. You're our daughter. *We're* supposed to protect and safeguard *you*, not the other way around," her dad told her.

"Your father's right. One hundred percent right," her mom stood staunchly with her husband.

"But you're my family. You mean everything to me, and I *want* to help you."

"Helping us is fine, but this is far and away beyond that, honey," her mom continued. "We've loved you being our employee, but it wasn't supposed to make you think that was a requirement of being our *child*."

"We've grown too dependent on her. She's always been a giver, and we've taken advantage," her dad put in, as if Kylie weren't there. He sounded so remorseful, too. She couldn't take it.

"No, you haven't."

"We have," her dad stated again. "I can see that now. You got involved with a *member of the mafia* over this, for heaven's sake. It has to stop. I'll put an ad in the paper today. I'm closing the business for today."

"But… isn't that overdoing it?" Kylie asked. The only time they'd ever closed in the past was due to flooding from a hurricane.

"*You* are our priority, Kylie. Not the business and not anything else. I'm sorry if we ever let you think otherwise. We're hiring from the outside while you focus on school. You should've been focusing on school instead of us anyway," her dad concluded, leaving her room as he tapped at something on his phone.

"Honey, tell me one more thing," her mother implored her, looking near tears herself. "Did this Tony guy do anything… inappropriate to you in exchange for that bargain you made with him?"

"No," Kylie hurried to disabuse her mother of that heinous notion. "Absolutely not. It wasn't like that. Not ever. He was… sweet. Compassionate. Funny. Creative."

"So that part wasn't some façade? You really did fall for him?"

"I know I misled you guys, but I wasn't misleading you at all when I told you I loved him. I thought he'd fallen for me, too, since that's what he said. But it couldn't have been true, could it? Not when he made the decision to do this extreme kamikaze attack rather than stay with me?"

"I don't know," her mom said as she sat next to her and extended an arm around her waist. Kylie laid her head on her shoulder. "I'll admit that he charmed me, had me believing he was the genuine article despite his family affiliations. But then again, when under duress, all of us can be guilty of making questionable decisions. Him especially, since he was raised in all that craziness. It must've been akin to being brought up in a cult."

"That's the thing, though," Kylie corrected her. "He never took part in any of the mob stuff until recently. Until after his mom died. He's an artist, Mom, and a violinist. He's a gentle soul who never should've been indoctrinated into the mafia lifestyle. And now, he's… he's gone."

Her mom hugged her close. Kylie felt so thankful for this, even though it did nothing to heal the giant hole in her heart.

"Do you know that for sure? That he really went through with it and… well… didn't survive?"

"Not for sure. But I do know that no matter what, he chose seeking vengeance over loving me. Even if he were to live through whatever he was planning, I can't forgive him for that. I'll never be able to trust him after this, not ever again."

CHAPTER SEVENTEEN

THIS TIME WHEN TONY TRAIPSED INTO THE HOSPITAL, IT WAS with an entirely different perspective. He understood what should be considered important and what should not, and when he checked at the information desk, he was told that Sandro had indeed been relocated to a regular room. Mentally, Tony tried to prepare himself for what he was about to see. He'd never been around anyone who had lost a limb before. He'd need to be calm and not react to however bad it was.

Plastering on what he hoped would be an expression that was at least partially cheerful, he crept through the open doorway. The room was far cozier than the Intensive Care ward had been. The door was a rich reddish-brown hardwood. The walls were a muted tan, and the tiled floors had been polished to a distinctive shine. The disinfectant odor that had been noticeable in the waiting area was much less so here, making for a more welcoming environment.

"There he is," Sandro announced, as if he were entering a party instead of a hospital room. "My baby brother. Are you all right?"

"I think that's my line, *fratello*." Attempting but failing to avoid looking at the left side of his body. Sandro was reclined on a series of pillows, so how he appeared with only a single arm wasn't readily apparent. Still, his skin tone had returned to its usual healthy coloring, and his eyes were clear and assessing.

"Perhaps."

"You seem chipper," Tony observed.

"I'm medicated, so the pain has mostly taken a vacation for now. Unless, of course, I move at all," he said all this with a jocular attitude, then sobered a bit, tipping his head downwards. This made an ebony lock of his hair slide forward onto his forehead. Tony approached and brushed it back for him, just like he had before. "It is going to be weird getting used to being so off balance physically. The arm both feels like it's there, and like it's not there. The prosthetist is supposed to be by today to fit a fake limb to my stub, so that's something to look forward to."

Tony's attention fixated on his brother's torso and over to where his right hand was and where his left hand was supposed to be. Sandro was gesticulating with his one remaining arm, and on his other side, his shoulder and part of his upper arm remained. They'd amputated it about six inches above his elbow.

It could've been worse, but to lose his appendage like that... what a nightmare.

"I'm so sorry, Sandro. I wish it had been me instead of you."

His brother frowned. "Don't say that, Antonio. The last thing I want is for you to be hurt."

"So, who did this? Will you tell me now? Giovanni? Gregorio or Luca? Some other Boccia?"

Alessandro's frown deepened even further. "What are you talking about?"

"About which Boccia shot you."

"It *wasn't* a Boccia who shot me."

"What?" Tony felt flabbergasted. "You specifically told me this was on the Boccias."

"I lied," Sandro confessed, sighing as he gazed directly into Tony's eyes. "That was a cover story. The truth is Pietro, Dante, and I were all out at the shooting range, and Dante was goofing around. His Glock went off when the barrel happened to be pointing in my direction."

Tony's jaw dropped open. "That little…" He didn't have a bad enough term for his irresponsible cousin. His negligence had cost Sandro dearly.

"It was an accident. I concealed the truth to keep Dante from being punished, but I didn't think it through very well. By the time I started to spout that story, I'd begun to feel woozy. I don't remember much after that. It seemed like a good idea at the time, but if I could retract that statement, I would. *Papà* would be hard on Dante, but he wouldn't kill him. At least, I don't think he would."

Tony shook his head. "And *Mamma*?"

"I think those things just poured out of me when I was sick because I've wondered about them ever since her accident. But the idea of the Boccias being involved? That's just speculation on my part or maybe wishful thinking. I have no proof of anything, and according to police reports, there's no evidence to support that theory."

"In all likelihood," he continued, "Bruno saw an animal—probably something like a deer—and swerved. He probably lost control and crashed, while the deer or whatever it was dashed off. But that version of events is highly unsatisfying to me. I wanted to be able to blame someone, you know? A person or group of people besides her driver. I wanted to have a reason to retaliate against her being taken away. Again, if I could go back and not say those words to you, I would."

Tony understood this all too well since he'd felt the exact same way. For so long in Tony's mind, his older brother had seemed untouchable, invincible. He'd revered and looked up to him all his life. To discover now—and in such a brutal, permanent manner—that his brother was just as fallible and imperfect as he himself was altered the way Tony looked at him. Sandro had been knocked from his pedestal, but the news wasn't negative. It meant he could relate to him even better. In that moment, he felt closer to his brother than he ever had.

"So the Boccias weren't to blame for anything," Tony summarized the whole situation.

"Not that I know of."

"Why are they our rivals, then?"

"Oh, that goes back a couple of generations," Sandro explained. "*Papà's* grandfather had some sort of beef with their grandfather, I think. I don't know precisely what transpired, though I believe that was when both our *famiglias* were still based in Chicago. Many of the larger and most powerful crime syndicates remain up there. The thing is, we haven't had an active outbreak of violence between the two clans since before either of us were born. Or even an escalation of hostility other than a few minor arguments and some posturing. *Papà* has been trying to broker negotiations with them lately which would mean working in concert with them. Hopefully, it will lead to a total cessation of any bad blood between us going forward."

"If I'd gone over there while our father was in the midst of those negotiations…" Tony trailed off.

"Let's just say it would've been a remarkably devastating idea where his long-term goals are concerned. He believes allying with them will be far more profitable overall. You know *Papà* and dollar signs. He's always eager to gain more of them, even if it means making nice with the Boccias."

Tony found a visitor's chair, which was cushioned unlike in the ICU. He plopped into it without any decorum whatsoever and couldn't have cared less. He needed to process all this new information and what it meant for him. What it meant for his *famiglia*. What the patriarch was doing could change the game forever.

He sat there in near silence for about an hour as Sandro snoozed on and off beside him. He was awakened when the healthcare worker came in to take measurements to fit his big brother with a new prosthetic arm.

"But he just had surgery," Tony protested to the middle-aged man.

"These take a while to make and your brother needs to get used to wearing it," the prosthetist said, his thick, salt-and-pepper hair sticking up in the back as he continued his ministrations unperturbed. "It's best to start fitting them as soon as possible."

Once he left, Tony stood and approached his brother's bed again. "Sandro, I don't think I'm cut out for this. I don't think I can take part in our crime syndicate."

Sandro offered him an authentically incandescent smile. "Music to my ears, *fratello*. That is the best news I've heard all day."

"You were right about me. I wanted to get closer to *Papà*, but *Papà* doesn't seem interested in getting closer to me."

"Don't take offense, Antonio. Viktor Menotti is a strong leader, but to say that he is father material is pushing it." It was the toughest thing Tony had ever heard his brother say about their father. "*Mamma* was the parent, the nurturer and caregiver. That's why losing her has been so difficult for us."

"And I got to spend far more time with her than you did."

"In her last few years, perhaps. But you have to remember that I had five years with her before you came along. *Papà* had not gotten a hold of me yet, so those were wonderful times. Happy and carefree. I don't resent you for coming along. I just wish sometimes that we hadn't been born into organized crime, that I might have been capable of exploring other occupational options."

"You could, you know," Tony pointed out. "You could break with tradition. What's *Papà* going to do? Threaten you?"

"He could cut off my other arm…" Sandro paused, then cracked a goofy grin. Tony grinned, too.

"That might prove unhelpful, though, since your ability to hold a gun would be severely limited."

"Good point," Sandro agreed. And soon both of them were laughing out loud at this morbid little experiment with gallows humor.

"I love you, *fratello*," Tony said, not wanting their only time saying this to each other to be due to his brother's delirium.

"I love you, Antonio. Now, are you going to ask me about your other problem?"

"You mean Kylie?" Sandro nodded sagely. "I sabotaged us. Good and proper. I'm fairly certain that she hates my guts now."

"Has she contacted you at all?"

Tony shook his head. Pietro, Dante, and Sandro had all reached out to him during his dangerous quest to seek retribution, but Kylie never had. "She told me if I went after the Boccias, we were over."

"And then you left to go after the Boccias anyway."

"I'm not overly smart, am I," Tony said, making it a statement rather than a query.

"Sometimes, no. But then that's true of all of us. You made an error in judgment. The question now is what are you going to do about it?"

"I've been a bit preoccupied with other concerns just in case you hadn't noticed."

"Yes, but you need a game plan. And it needs to be airtight."

"I have been pondering a few possibilities," Tony admitted.

"Like what?"

"Like groveling."

"Groveling isn't going to cut it, Antonio. You need to both apologize and prove to her that you won't do something like that again. Unless this is nothing serious, nothing more than a fling."

"It's much more than a fling. I love her. I want to be with her for the rest of my life."

"Well, it's time to think outside of the box, then. Pull out all the stops. Go big or go home," Sandro quipped.

"Have any more useful idioms or analogies?"

"Fair enough. Do you know what she likes?"

"Yes."

"Then, give her as much of that as you can."

He knew Sandro was right. Whatever he did would have

to be something spectacular but also heartfelt. It'd been so easy to fall in love with her, and she'd seemed to fall just as easily. Surely, he could convince her that he'd merely made a mistake, and things could go back to the way they were. He thought of how fantastic it'd felt to have her by his side in that waiting room, how she'd stood by him. Like his mother, Kylie was a devoted and sympathetic type.

He felt certain if he tried hard enough, he could win her back. It would just be a matter of making his case with her.

CHAPTER EIGHTEEN

Four weeks had elapsed since Kylie had seen Tony Menotti, and while she'd heard from him, she hadn't replied. Still, it'd been difficult not to respond to that first text she received from him.

Tony: *Bellisima*, I didn't go through with it. I didn't go to the Boccias. I was being a hotheaded fool, and I'm sorry.

She'd been so tempted to call him, or to at least text him back. But she'd abstained. She'd had to for the sake of her own sanity. She had so much she wanted to scream at him about. How he'd broken her heart. How he'd made the worst choice imaginable when she'd desperately needed him to make the right one. She wanted to yell at him until she was blue in the face, to order him not to call her *bellisima* anymore, because he'd officially lost the privilege.

But she also wanted to race into his arms.

What she really needed to do was take him out of her contacts, or better, to block him from her phone entirely. Yet she couldn't seem to make herself do it. Even though she felt like everything between them was finished, it hurt too much to make that final decision, to take that last step.

There were a gazillion books, movies, and songs about the pain of breaking up with someone, but she'd never fully understood what they were talking about before. She did now, though. Way too well. After seeing that first text from Tony, she'd slumped on her bed in relief that he was alive, then spent the rest of the day in an annoyed tizzy, unable to concentrate on a single solitary thing. Since then, he'd texted her many times.

Tony: I miss you.

Tony: I love you. I never stopped.

Tony: I really am sorry, and I'm going to fix this, I promise.

Tony: Would you please text me back with an emoji or something, so I at least know you're receiving these?

She'd created this rule for herself that she wouldn't break or give in to him. That she wouldn't deign to answer him no matter what. But at that last text, she'd broken her rule for long enough to send him some emojis just like he'd wanted.

Kylie: (red angry face emoji) (broken heart emoji)

That pretty much summed it all up.

She felt almost sure that he had no idea how much he'd destroyed her when he'd trotted off like he had. There had been a fiercely rational and wary voice inside of her that had objected to the relationship with him since the beginning. It'd been so small and so quiet that she'd blown it off like a piece of dandelion fluff, but look where that had gotten her.

Every time she went into her parents' business, she thought of him. Every time she saw a black sportscar, she stopped and squinted at it, checking to see if it was his sleek little Audi. Every time she passed the Stuffed Potato or the fountain by the Law School—which was daily—she thought of him. He seemed to be everywhere, even in his absence.

Because she'd taken her mom and dad's advice and taken a full course load at UNT for the first time ever, she couldn't escape these unhappy reminders. It got to the point of her journeying out of her way across campus, taking more indirect routes that took longer to traverse just to avoid seeing as much of these places as possible. She'd just sat down for her first day in her new computer-based systems class when she kept catching these whiffs of him.

She'd craned her neck, looking for him in every last seat before realizing that one of the guys who'd sat behind her must be wearing the same cologne Tony used. Since her eyes were getting all prickly and her throat was closing up, she'd stood and gone to the far side of the room, even though she always sat front and center. She just couldn't take smelling his scent when he wasn't there.

Still, she did her best to focus exclusively on her classes. Her parents had hired not one but two new hires to help out at work. Kylie now only did one four-hour shift on Sunday afternoons at her mom and dad's insistence. It'd been so long since she'd had that much free time—even though she spent the majority of it studying and doing homework—that it felt almost outlandish to have so much choice. One day when everything was caught up, she decided to go visit her uncle.

She'd grown up envying her Uncle Kyle for his amazing life, and seeing him so debilitated was hard. He'd had so much life in him just a couple of years ago, yet now, he was deteriorating rapidly. Still, since she'd only visited him once right after they'd moved here, she felt it was her due diligence to suck it up and be there for him. Even if he didn't know it.

As her taxi pulled up to the Caruth Haven Court Nursing Facility, Kylie took in its immaculately kept grounds and fresh, pale pink brickwork outlining the three-story structure. The place had lots of green landscaping and curved brick pathways that wound gently across the yard. The communal areas of the bottom story had large, clean windows to let the light in, and there was an assortment of old-growth trees visible through them.

Outside the main entrance were autumn decorations like pumpkins, hay bales, and even friendly-looking scarecrows in colorful garb. Along one side of the building was a white fence that highlighted an outdoor porch where residents could sit outside in the shade and enjoy the weather in comfy green chairs. With some members of staff with them, of course.

As such places went, it was as nice as anyone could make it.

When she meandered in, Kylie was greeted by a white-haired receptionist wearing a broad smile. Her name tag said Gladys. "How may I help you, dear?"

"Hi, I'm Kylie Cormier. I'm here to see my uncle, Kyle Wentworth."

"Ah, Kyle. Such a life he's lived." Gladys brought her hands together in front of her in a silent clap, her eyes becoming vibrant. "On his good days, he used to tell us all about it."

Used to. Kylie didn't miss the past tense that the lady had utilized in her speech.

"Does he ever have good days anymore?"

"Oh, well, sometimes. I can't deny that those are growing fewer and farther between, but when he has them, he lights up the room."

Kylie had no doubt of that.

"Let me escort you to him," Gladys concluded, leading Kylie through the facility.

When they arrived in his room, he was absent, but she and Gladys could hear some shuffling and muffled voices in his attached restroom. "I'm sure he'll be out soon. Make yourself at home, dear. Let us know if you need anything at all."

"I will. Thank you."

Left alone, Kylie perused the many photos her mother had affixed to her uncle's walls. She'd gone through his picture albums and stuck as many of them as she could to every vertical surface. Her reasoning had been sound.

"Not only does it make his room more interesting and less lonely, it also might help to jog his memory."

Even if this didn't prove to be true, Kylie still liked the effect. She could spend at least an hour just looking at each individual photograph and marveling at what an exciting life her uncle had lived prior to his diagnosis. Kylie had once watched a documentary where dozens of elderly people had been interviewed. The interviewer had asked if they had any regrets, and a substantial portion of them had said that they wished they'd taken more risks and not played it so safe.

"I was always shy and tentative about the choices I made," one lady had said. "I wish I'd made myself get out of my comfort zone more."

"My folks had certain expectations of me, and I was always so afraid of disappointing them," another man had answered. "I wish I'd done more of what I wanted, that I'd taken more chances."

Kyle had not been one of those people. He'd lived his life to the fullest amount conceivable, and Kylie felt so proud of him for taking the bull by the horns, so to speak. She sincerely doubted her uncle had any regrets.

The door to the bathroom banged open as her uncle pushed through on a walker.

"Oh," said the attending nurse, a plump, dark-skinned lady in lavender scrubs with a compassionate smile. "Looks like you have company today."

"Bettina," he called out to Kylie, grinning. Bettina was her mother's name, but she didn't have the heart to correct him.

"Hi, Kyle," she said instead, playing along and struggling to keep smiling. His appearance had grown so much more haggard than it had been.

"Oh, look at you, all down in the dumps."

"I'm fine," she fibbed.

"Well, honey, I told you to go back to him."

Kylie gawked at him. "What do you mean?"

"Reggie," he spoke her father's name. This astonished her. To Kylie's knowledge, her mother and father had never broken up. They'd fallen for each other young and had stayed together always. It'd been a perfect little fairy tale. Or so she'd thought. Of course, Kyle may just be confused again. "You have to forgive him, Bett. I know he made a mistake, but we all do sometimes. He's a good man, and you were so happy when you were with him. Go talk to him, okay? Work things out. You'll be glad you did."

Kylie felt as if she'd fallen down Alice's rabbit hole. She knew her uncle was talking about her parents, but his words chipped away at the ice she'd encased her broken heart in. It was as if he was giving her advice about Tony, and his references were accurate enough to be eerie.

They spent a couple of hours together, mostly him talking and her listening. He told the same stories she'd heard many times over and over, but she just let him go on. She knew on his bad days he'd be bedridden and basically catatonic, so she didn't want to waste this precious time where he was almost himself.

When he hugged her goodbye, he said something else that gave her pause. "That man loves you, Kylie." *Kylie*, not

Bettina. She goggled at him. He and her mom were brother and sister and had identical eyes, the same aqua blue that she'd inherited. "He deserves a second chance."

Right before she left, the Activities Director came by with a small digital camera. "Would you like a picture of you and your uncle?" she asked. "I'll make two copies so you can both have one."

"That's very kind. Yes, that would be awesome."

The lady snapped the pic, then disappeared into her office. When she materialized again, she had two matching images printed out with color ink and printed on photo paper. "Here you are. They came out great, didn't they? Kyle, I'm putting this one right next to your headboard." Somehow, she found a blank spot on the wall and filled it.

Kylie glanced down at the picture and felt her eyes burn. She and her uncle had their arms around one another and were smiling just like in the old days before his dementia had started to take him over. Sniffling and giving the Activities Director an impromptu hug on her way out, Kylie started to tell the taxi driver to take her home, but instead, she changed her mind. She wanted her parents to see this most recent image of Kyle, especially since her uncle looked so good in it. So she gave him the address for Cormier's Cleaning and Alterations instead.

Her dad was busy at the counter when she came in, so she went to the sewing room to see her mom. The instant she showed her mom the photograph, tears filled her eyes. "Oh, Kylie. Thank you for going. This makes my day."

"Kylie," her dad snuck his head in the back and hollered over the noise of the washing machines. "Someone's here asking for you."

Since she no longer worked there much, she was puzzled. Who would come looking for her here? She stepped out to the front to see an unfamiliar man in a tuxedo with a red bow tie and vest.

"Ms. Kylie Cormier?" the man asked in a loud, rather theatrical voice.

"Yes."

"This is for you." He yanked out a miniature harmonica, blew out a note, lifted a piece of card stock, and began to sing, "*Bellisima*, you have the most beautiful eyes... *Bellisima*, your love I can't deny... *Bellisima*, I don't want to say goodbye... *Bellisima*, come outside for a big surprise."

Both Kylie and her dad stared at the man who'd just delivered a singing telegram. Kylie hadn't even known singing telegrams were still a thing. Her mom appeared at her side right at the tail end of it. "What's going on out here?"

"I have no idea," Kylie said, but she couldn't be clueless as to the sender. Only one person on the planet had ever called her very beautiful in Italian.

"I've been instructed to take the lovely Kylie outside," the singer said, hand outstretched for hers.

Feeling a little surly now, she refused to take the man's hand, but she did follow him outside. And there in the parking lot in the same location was another hot air balloon. She didn't know how Tony had done this, but somehow this new balloon had been created to look like an enormous note. It said:

I'm out, Kylie, and I love you. Please forgive me.

Then, she noticed that below the balloon stood the man whom she hadn't seen in over a month. Tony approached, wearing a contrite expression. Instead of his customary tailored suit he'd donned an exquisitely refined tuxedo. It put the tux the singing telegram guy wore to shame. In his hands, he held a huge bouquet of roses which included every color of the rainbow.

"I mean it," he said.

She shook her head, perplexed. "I don't understand."

"I'm out of the business of my *famiglia*. I'm out of organized crime. Being a part of the mob cost me you, so I'm never going back. It's not worth it. I want nothing to do with it anymore. The only thing I want is you."

CHAPTER NINETEEN

As Tony regarded Kylie, she folded her arms over her chest. "It's nice that you're out, but that doesn't change what you did."

"I know. I know that, and I'm sorry. I'm so sorry, *bellisima*. I'll do whatever it takes to make things right again."

But despite everything he was saying, she seemed unmoved. Glowering at him, she didn't budge an inch, even when he offered her the bouquet of roses. His heart sank. It'd taken him a month to orchestrate this, and now it all seemed for naught.

"What do you say?" he prompted her, hoping against hope. But her response didn't exactly fill him with joy.

"I don't know, Tony. Singing telegrams and grand gestures are nice and everything. But this is a lot to get over."

"What do you want? I'll get it for you. Anything. The same goes for whatever you might wish me to do. Do you want me on my knees begging?" He dropped to them right there on the pavement in front of her. The chunky blacktop was tearing up both his tux and the skin over his kneecaps, but he didn't care. She had to comprehend how serious his intentions were. He'd never been more serious in his life. "Please take me back, Kylie. *Please*."

Her father appeared behind her, his arms over his chest in a mirror image of his daughter. The hateful look on his face gave Tony all the information about him that he needed to know. This wasn't working, and Tony didn't know what else to do. Feeling desperate, he stood back up and addressed her father.

"Sir, I swear to you that I mean what I say. I've left that life of crime behind totally. I can't control the *famiglia* I was born into, but I can control whether I participate or not, and I'm not. Not ever again."

"What about your father? Don't you feel like you owe him some type of allegiance?"

"I did at one time, that is true. But the only thing pursuing that did was ruin what I had with Kylie. I love your daughter more than anything on this Earth, and I'll die protecting her if need be."

"You hurt her," her dad went on.

"I know."

"You broke her heart."

"I know, and I'm so sorry." This was excruciating. What more could he say? How many more promises did her father want Tony to make? "Please believe me."

At length, he nodded, though he didn't loosen his stance any. "I'm inclined to, but it doesn't matter if I believe you or not. What matters is if Kylie does."

Agreed. Tony just didn't know how to make that happen.

Reggie Cormier turned and left, leaving Tony and Kylie alone once more. He scrutinized her, noticing that she was staring at the hot air balloon. Or, no, she wasn't. She seemed to be staring off into space.

"He's a good man," she muttered to herself. "We all make mistakes sometimes, and everyone deserves a second chance."

"Kylie?"

"All right. I've made a decision. I've decided *that's* not going to work."

"What's not going to work?" he asked, wondering if she was feeling okay. She was behaving quite out of character based on the Kylie he knew.

"This whole 'Kylie' business. It has to stop."

More baffled than ever, Tony reached out and took her hand. "You have me at a loss, I'm afraid."

"You know that was Dad's own version of giving his blessing," she said, still looking off into the distance. Since all she seemed to be speaking in was non sequiturs, he merely observed her, hoping something would start making sense.

At last, she met his gaze, her aqua blue eyes connecting to his. Her features softened and warmed as they stared at one another, and then, she raised each of her hands to the sides of his face. Tugging him toward her, she pulled him down until his lips made contact with hers, and everything that had been going topsy-turvy in his life righted itself in one fell swoop.

Bracketing his arms around her, he embraced her, relishing having her so near, relishing knowing that everything was going to work out after all. She broke the kiss, and he missed her immediately, but then she leaned against his shoulder, staying close.

"I love you, Tony."

"I love you, *bellisima*. More than I can ever express."

"That's better."

"What is?"

"*Bellisima*. I've decided I don't like you calling me what everyone else does. I'm Kylie to my family, my friends, my teachers, even *strangers*, but to you…"

"To me, you'll always be 'very beautiful.'"

"Yes," she sighed out, a smile in her voice.

"What were you talking about before? All that 'good man' and 'second chances' stuff?" he asked, realizing she'd been leading up to something he hadn't been able to absorb then.

"Just following some suggestions from my beloved uncle."

"You mean the one with—"

"With dementia," she finished for him. "Yes. The interesting thing about that is despite his infirmity, he still managed to offer me that sage advice. He called me by my mom's name, but I now have no doubt whatsoever that his message was meant for me."

"Perhaps he was speaking to you through his soul."

"It's entirely possible," she agreed.

"It's really quite fascinating to think about," he told her, remembering the poignant conversation he'd shared with his deceased mother. In actuality, Kylie's discussion with her mentally ill uncle wasn't all that different.

"It is, isn't it?"

"*Bellisima*," he began.

"Yes, Tony."

"Thank you for forgiving me, for coming back to me." Embarrassingly, his voice came out somewhat croaky. But he felt so much gratitude right then, he couldn't help it. "I don't know what I would do if I had to keep going without you. This past month has been…"

"Not fun."

"Exceedingly not fun."

"Then, let's never separate like that again."

"Deal."

She snickered. "You know the last time we made a deal, it led to us falling for each other."

"That's true. It's the best deal I ever made until this one. *Bellisima*?"

"Hmmmm?"

"Would you like to go on another hot air balloon ride with me?"

She tipped up her chin and smiled up at him with those sparkling eyes and dimples that he adored. Someday, he wanted their kids to inherit both of those features. "Can't think of a single thing I'd like better."

EPILOGUE

One Year Later

"HERE, HONEY, HOLD STILL WHILE I PUT THIS ONE LAST PIN in… okay, got it. What do you think?" her mom asked as she lifted the mirror around so Kylie could see her hair. It was the perfect combination of flowing down around her shoulders and curly updo. She loved it. But then, her mom had always been extremely nimble with her fingers.

"You're awesome, Mom."

"I know," she said, then giggled. There'd been a lot of giggling today, in fact. Between nerves, Shelley visiting from the Big Easy, and all the impending excitement, it was hard *not* to giggle.

This day only exemplified the many different aspects of her life that were awesome. Because she'd gone from part-time classes to an accelerated program, she'd graduated from UNT Dallas with her accounting degree in May. It'd been intense—she'd basically eaten, drunk, and lived her textbooks—but she'd made it. It'd felt so rewarding to complete such an important accomplishment.

Her parents' business was flourishing far more than it had in New Orleans, and much of that was due to their new marketing guru. The guy had revolutionized their ads and brought so many fresh customers to their door that they were considering opening a second location. His unique charcoal artwork combined with his ability to play his own soundtrack over the ad with his violin made for ads that stood out from the crowd.

Also, that marketing guru? His name was Tony. The Menottis' loss had turned into her and her family's gain. Sadly, Tony had been disowned by his father, the patriarch of their organized crime clan. He didn't see much of his dad anymore, but in truth, he really didn't seem all that broken up about it. One person he had kept in touch with was his brother, Alessandro. Those two stayed in constant communication.

Kylie grinned just thinking about the man she loved. The past year and a half together had been the best of Kylie's life, and with any luck, their future would be even better. She touched up her lipstick and examined the rest of her makeup. Kylie had never been much of a cosmetics girl, so she felt a bit out of her depth. Luckily, Shelley lived for mascara, eye shadow, and foundation.

"Are you sure this shade works for me, Shell? It seems kind of wild."

"It's wild because it matches your fuchsia color scheme. Relax. Even if it didn't match, you can pull it off. Besides,

Tony thinks you're beautiful no matter what you're wearing on your lips."

"If you say so."

She then regarded her gown. Brilliant white lace over satin greeted her as she peered at her reflection. It was floor length, form-fitting, and beaded with pearls at the bodice. The top of the back was open with pearl strands criss-crossing back and forth in a pattern that reminded Kylie of faraway lands, knights, princesses, and fairy tales. Similar pearl strands had been braided into her hair. The effect, with her mom and best friend's help, was magical.

"Kylie," her dad knocked at the door. "How close are you to being ready?"

She gave herself yet another onceover. "I'm close." How many times could she worry out loud about her lipstick? "No, never mind, I'm ready now. Let's do this."

As she stepped out of the ladies' dressing room, she tapped her way out in the heels she planned to kick off the second the ceremony was over. She'd chosen these death traps because they put her at a much better height to kiss Tony, but actually wearing the crazy things? She imagined this must be why she'd never worn them before. When she opened her own CPA practice, she was wearing *flats*. Or maybe even tennis shoes, she hadn't decided yet.

Speaking of her CPA practice, she'd already picked out the perfect location. There was a tiny office two doors down from her parents' dry-cleaning establishment, which would suit her just fine. Its current renters were leaving in two months, which, since it was only September, would give her plenty of time to prepare. She should be able to get everything situated during the holidays so she could be ready for tax season. Her career, just like so many other aspects of her life, was falling into place.

Once she lined up next to her dad, he brought her arm around his. The music that had been playing so melodically with the acoustics in the expansive grand hall of the Dallas Museum of Art became louder. It caused a frisson of anticipation to zap through her from head to pointy-toed, stiletto shoes. "Just lean on me," her dad whispered in her ear, as if he could read just how thrilled yet jittery she was. "I'll keep you upright."

"Thanks, Dad."

Slowly, they walked toward the head of the space. At the top of the room near the backdrop of a ginormous window dotted with multi-colored glass sculptures suspended from the ceiling stood the officiant they'd hired. In front of her, Shelley sashayed up the aisle with Sandro—she stood at his right side so they could go up arm in arm—and as soon as the two of them shifted slightly, she caught sight of him.

The man she'd be marrying today.

He was always so dapper in a tuxedo, and as their eyes latched onto each other's, her breathing hitched at the depth of love she could see so plainly in his butterscotch eyes. This man had left his family legacy behind to be with her, had estranged himself from his father to be with her, had abandoned a trust worth *billions* to be with her. If she ever doubted his love for her after all that, then she didn't deserve him.

Their wedding party was miniscule. There were only she and Tony, her parents, Shelley, Sandro, Sandro's fiancée, Angelia, and the officiant, but that was fine by Kylie. All the people she loved most in the world were in attendance, and they were a tightly knit group. Sandro had met Angelia about a year ago, and they'd just gotten engaged two weeks previous. Despite the loss of his arm, Sandro was doing phenomenally well.

He'd largely pulled away from the crime organization he'd once been groomed to take over, telling his father that he preferred to stay within the umbrella of the law. Kylie suspected that Viktor Menotti had not been happy about this, but what could he do? Both of his sons were their own men, and short of snuffing out the lives of his progeny, he was faced with letting them live as they preferred.

Kylie offered up a little prayer in the hopes that her Uncle Kyle could see them from wherever he was in heaven. He'd passed six months ago peacefully in his sleep.

"Dearly beloved," the officiant started off, "we are gathered here today to celebrate the deep and abiding love of Kylie and Tony. Love is what elevates us, what connects us and brings us together. We were created from love and are made of love. Nothing can tarnish the purest forms of love, and when two people are united by it, nothing in this world can separate them."

Turning to Kylie, he said, "Kylie Alexandra Cormier, do you take this man to have and to hold, for richer or for poorer, in sickness and in health, to love, honor, cherish, and respect for all of eternity?"

"I do," she said, holding Tony's gaze without pause.

The officiant turned to Tony. "Antonio Vincenzo Menotti, do you take this woman to have and to hold, for richer or for poorer, in sickness and in health, to love, honor, cherish, and respect for all of eternity?"

"I do, *bellisima*," he told her with discernible emotion in his voice.

"The wedding ring represents your everlasting devotion to one another. Its shape, a circle, illustrates how boundless, how endless love is meant to be. It is infinite, stronger than it looks, and displays how the feelings you share are unbreakable. With that in mind, at this time you will give one another rings to demonstrate to the world that you have pledged to spend your lives together."

Kylie twisted around to Shelley, who offered her Tony's wedding band, a silver titanium one inset with a swirling blue pattern.

"Place your groom's ring on the third finger of his left hand and repeat after me, 'With this ring, I thee wed.'"

"With this ring, I thee wed." She tried not to tremble for fear of dropping her soon-to-be husband's wedding band, but the momentousness of the occasion wasn't lost on her. Still, she managed to slip the ring on without incident.

"Now, place your bride's ring on the third finger of her left hand and repeat after me, 'With this ring, I thee wed.'"

Kylie glanced down at the wedding ring set Tony had proposed to her with ten months prior. It, too, was cast of silver titanium with a two-carat round diamond at the center and surrounded by a series of smaller diamonds around the band. On either side of the solitaire were triangular aquamarines that matched the swirling color in her husband's.

The jeweler had soldered the engagement ring and wedding band together. It was dainty, flattering on her hand, and absolutely perfect. And when Tony echoed the officiant's words, he gazed into her eyes while performing the action of sliding it on, the intense adoration and dedication he felt for her more than clear.

"Then, with the powers vested in me by the great state of Texas," the officiant grinned as he spoke, "I now pronounce you husband and wife. Mr. Menotti, you may kiss your bride."

Belting his arms around her tightly, as if he couldn't get her close enough, Tony's lips met hers. Then, without warning, he dipped her backwards, never once breaking the seal of their kiss. Her eyes went wide with surprise, then closed, because she trusted him to hold her, to catch her, and to never again let her go.

I HOPE you enjoyed reading *A Change of Plans for the Youngest Son*. Writing about bad boys for a clean and wholesome series has been fun and enlightening. Of course these characters aren't perfect by any means. They have flaws. They have faults. They're not all necessarily nice. But I've always believed that every person is redeemable if they want to be. I'm thrilled to have found enough redeemable men to match them up with their perfect matches in this series.

Our next story of redemption is the story of a second chance at romance for a couple who had ended badly. They've done well with their lives since the break up, so maybe getting back together wasn't really an option. Be sure to follow their renewed relationship to see if there's a chance for them.

A Rude Awakening for the Ambition Ex-Boyfriend is book 5 in the series,

Dr. Amber Crawford has dedicated her life to caring for others and she's determined to leave a legacy that her mother would be proud of. This path, though noble and worthy, leaves no time for a love life. Truthfully, she's okay with that since the only man she ever cared for shredded her heart and left her in the gritty Texas dust.

When Amber runs into hunky Troy Sykes almost ten years later she wants to vanish and pretend he never existed. But before she can sneak away, he sees her and it's too late. And just like that, she's agreed to have dinner with him.

He turns on his signature wit and charm and she's soon under spell again. He seems different than the college boy who dumped her without a look back. She believes he's matured and learned the value of treating others well. He's a respected attorney, so of course he gets it now.

Just as Amber is falling for him again, he unceremoniously breaks things off. He's ruined her trust in him twice.

Bitter and angry, she throws herself back into her work. Knowing she should have trusted her instincts, she takes a breath and moves on.

But when Troy's career and life takes a monumental dive, he turns to her for help. She's insulted he's asking for her help. The nerve of this man!

Her conscience won't allow her to ignore someone who needs help.

Will she allow Troy to destroy her as he tries to pull himself together? Or will this experience bring them together as he finally sees what he should have seen all along?

~

FIND *A RUDE Awakening for the Ambitions Ex-Boyfriend* on Amazon.

~

CHECK OUT THIS FREE COWBOY ROMANCE!

If you enjoyed this sweet cowboy romance, you'll want to read *Finding Her Cowboy*! This story is where two best selling series meet with another heartwarming love story!

This stand alone story is an enemies to lovers whirlwind romance set in small town Texas where Thatcher Ranch and Bolton Ranch meet.

The Brothers of Thatcher Ranch series and the Billionaire Ranchers series comes together with cameo appearances by characters in each one.

Get a taste of each sweet romance series when city girl Adelaide and cowboy Maddox fall in love in the rancher's world Addy shouldn't fit into, but does.

Tap here to get your copy of Finding Her Cowboy

Made in the USA
Middletown, DE
23 September 2022

11068627R00116